DC

TEEN TITANS GO!™

Cover design by Elaine Lopez-Levine.

Little, Brown and Company
Hachette Book Group
1290 Avenue of the Americas, New York, NY 10104
Visit us at LBYR.com

First Edition: June 2018

Little, Brown and Company is a division of Hachette Book Group, Inc.
The Little, Brown and Company name and logo are trademarks
of Hachette Book Group, Inc.

The publisher is not responsible for websites (or their content)
that are not owned by the publisher.

Library of Congress Control Number 2018940700

ISBNs: 978-0-316-47614-0 (paper over board),
978-0-316-47616-4 (ebook), 978-0-316-47615-7 (ebook),
978-0-316-47617-1 (ebook)

Printed in the United States of America

LSC-C

10 9 8 7 6 5 4 3 2 1

The World-Famous Guidebook

by Brandon T. Snider

LITTLE, BROWN AND COMPANY
New York   Boston

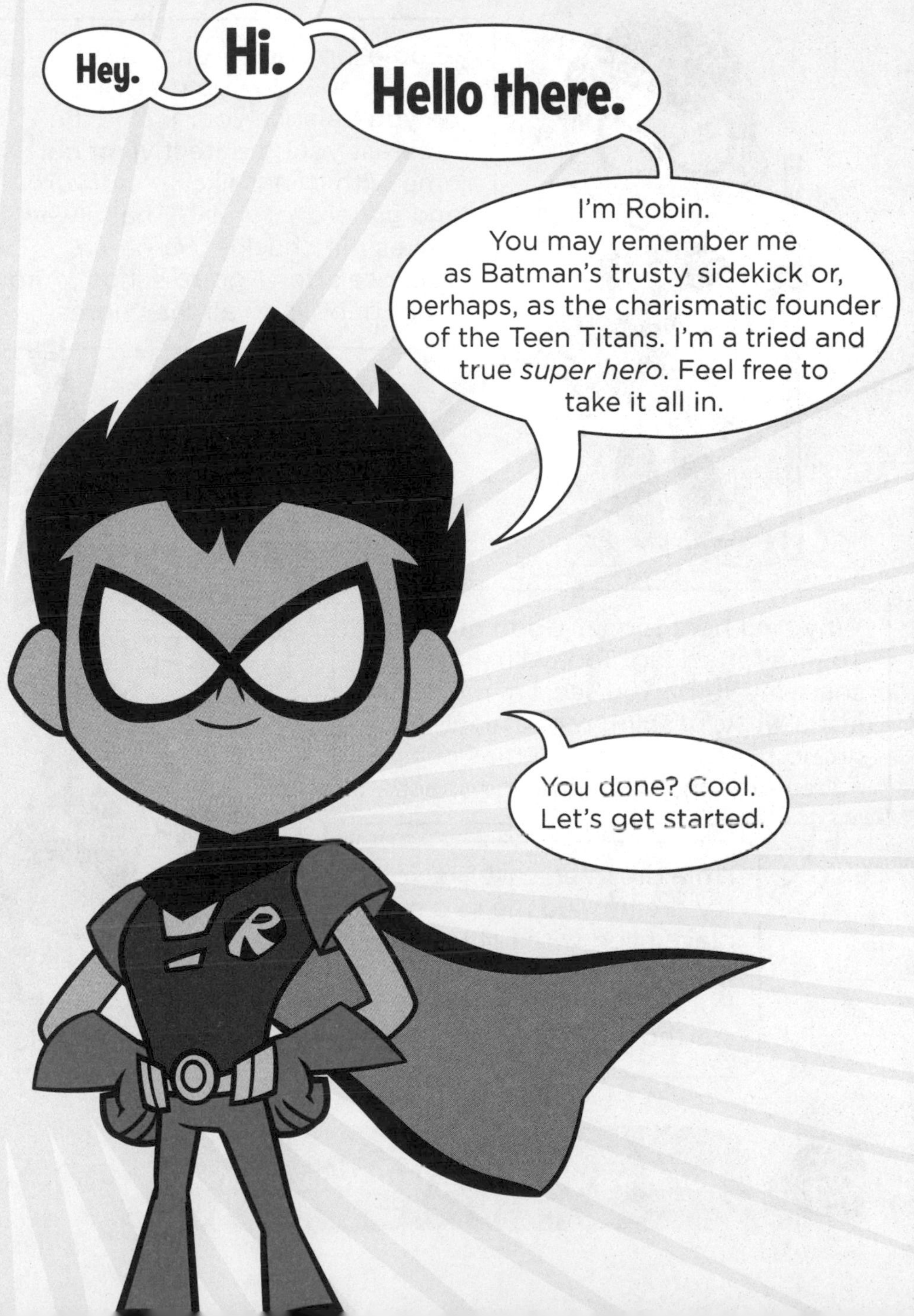
Hey.
Hi.
Hello there.
I'm Robin. You may remember me as Batman's trusty sidekick or, perhaps, as the charismatic founder of the Teen Titans. I'm a tried and true *super hero*. Feel free to take it all in.
You done? Cool. Let's get started.

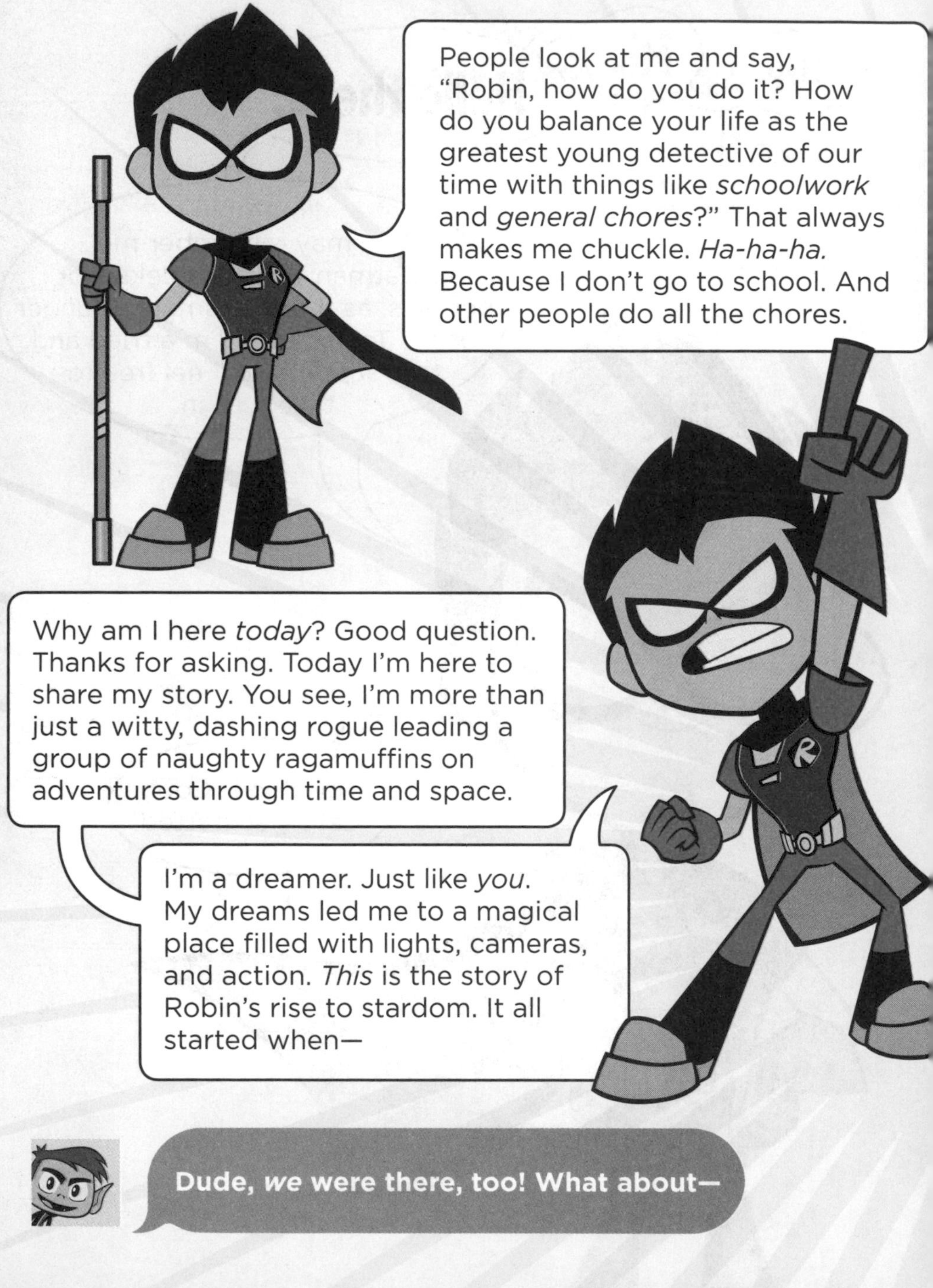

People look at me and say, "Robin, how do you do it? How do you balance your life as the greatest young detective of our time with things like *schoolwork* and *general chores*?" That always makes me chuckle. *Ha-ha-ha.* Because I don't go to school. And other people do all the chores.
Why am I here *today*? Good question. Thanks for asking. Today I'm here to share my story. You see, I'm more than just a witty, dashing rogue leading a group of naughty ragamuffins on adventures through time and space.
I'm a dreamer. Just like *you*. My dreams led me to a magical place filled with lights, cameras, and action. *This* is the story of Robin's rise to stardom. It all started when—
Dude, *we* were there, too! What about—

Beast Boy, I'm trying to tell my story here. A timeless tale of intrigue, danger, and mystery. The highest highs and the lowest lows. It's probably *the biggest thing to ever happen to me in my entire life*—that is, at least until I become Nightwing.

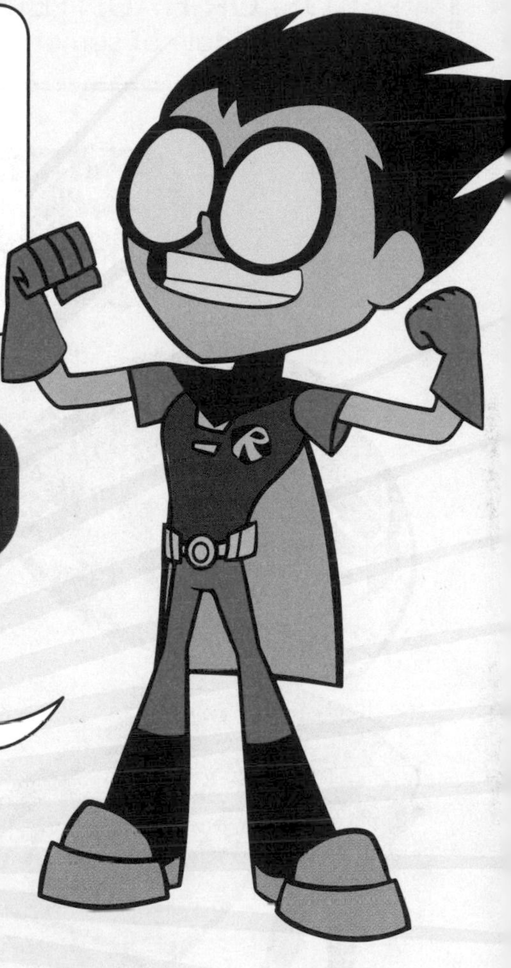

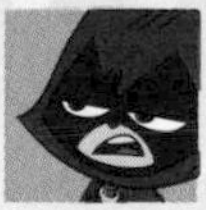

Said the orphan who lost his parents in a circus mishap.

What can I say? My ability to process tragic events is enviable. Staying calm and positive while facing down numerous hardships is my strongest suit. *But I digress....*

Dude, let's get a buttload of tacos, decorate Titans Tower like a haunted house from space, and then throw the biggest P-A-R-T-Y in the history of the WORLD!

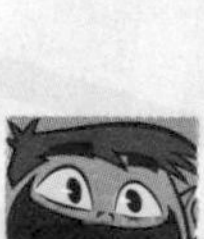

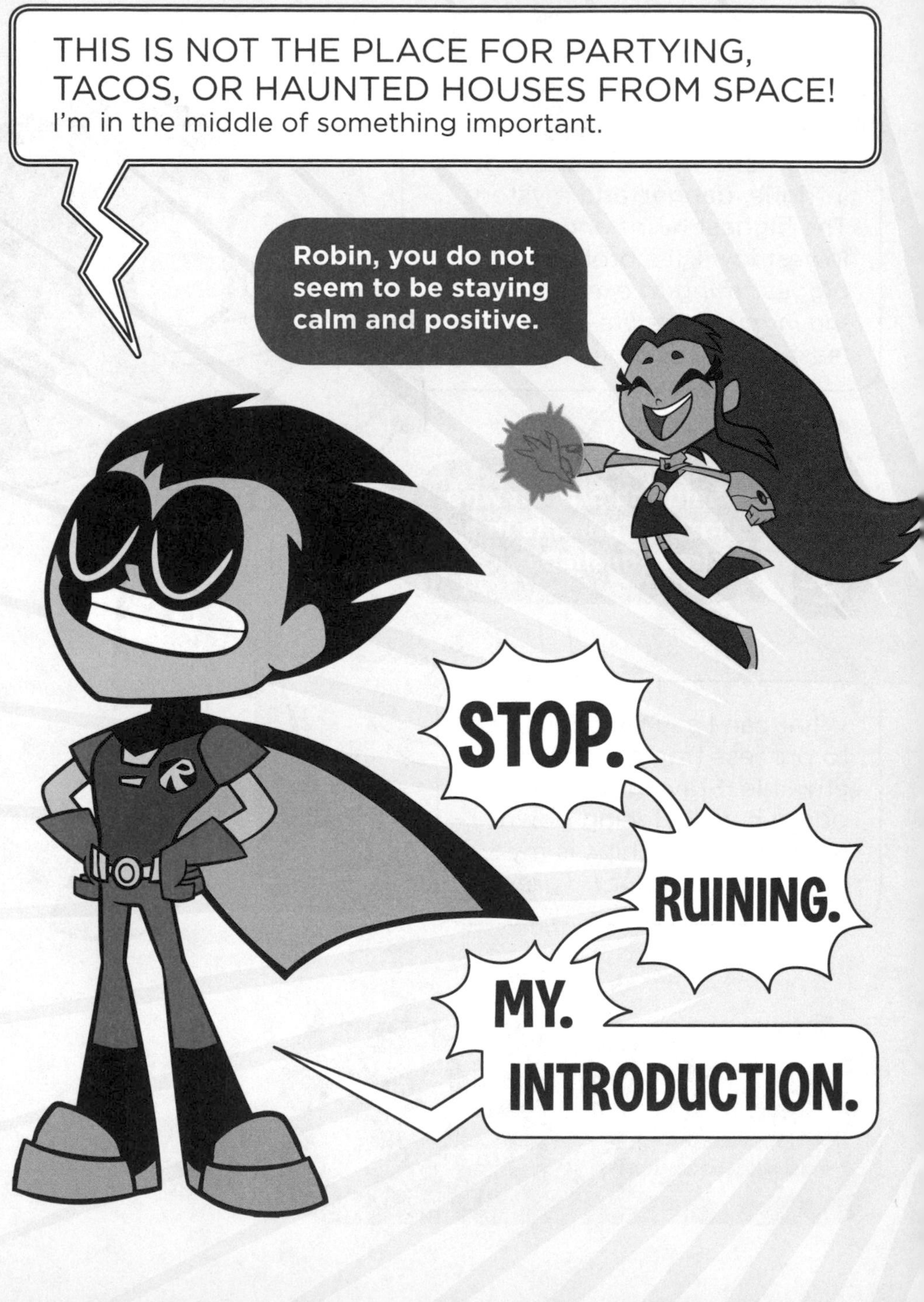
THIS IS NOT THE PLACE FOR PARTYING, TACOS, OR HAUNTED HOUSES FROM SPACE! I'm in the middle of something important.
Robin, you do not seem to be staying calm and positive.
STOP.
RUINING.
MY.
INTRODUCTION.

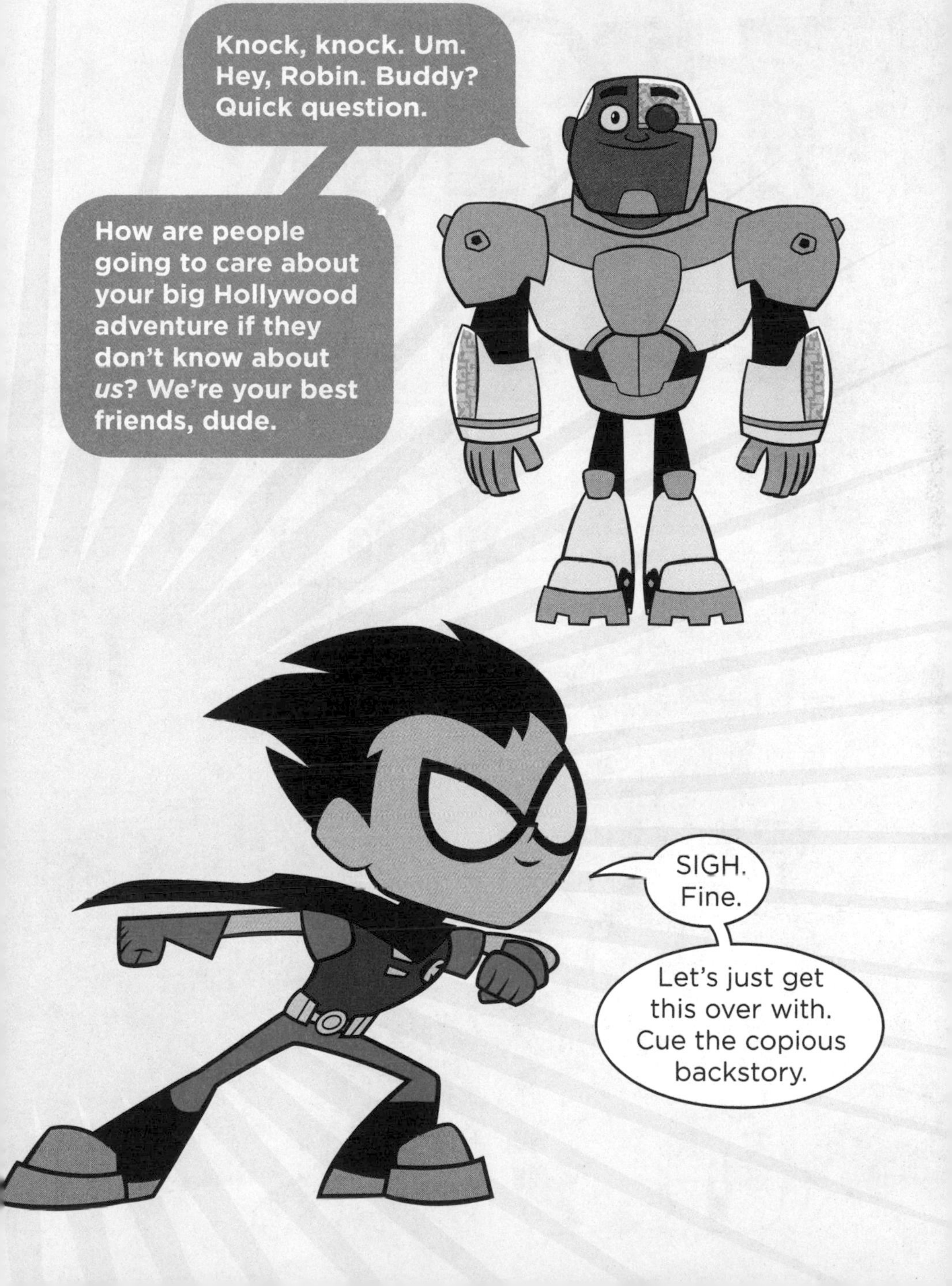
Knock, knock. Um. Hey, Robin. Buddy? Quick question.
How are people going to care about your big Hollywood adventure if they don't know about *us*? We're your best friends, dude.
SIGH. Fine.
Let's just get this over with. Cue the copious backstory.

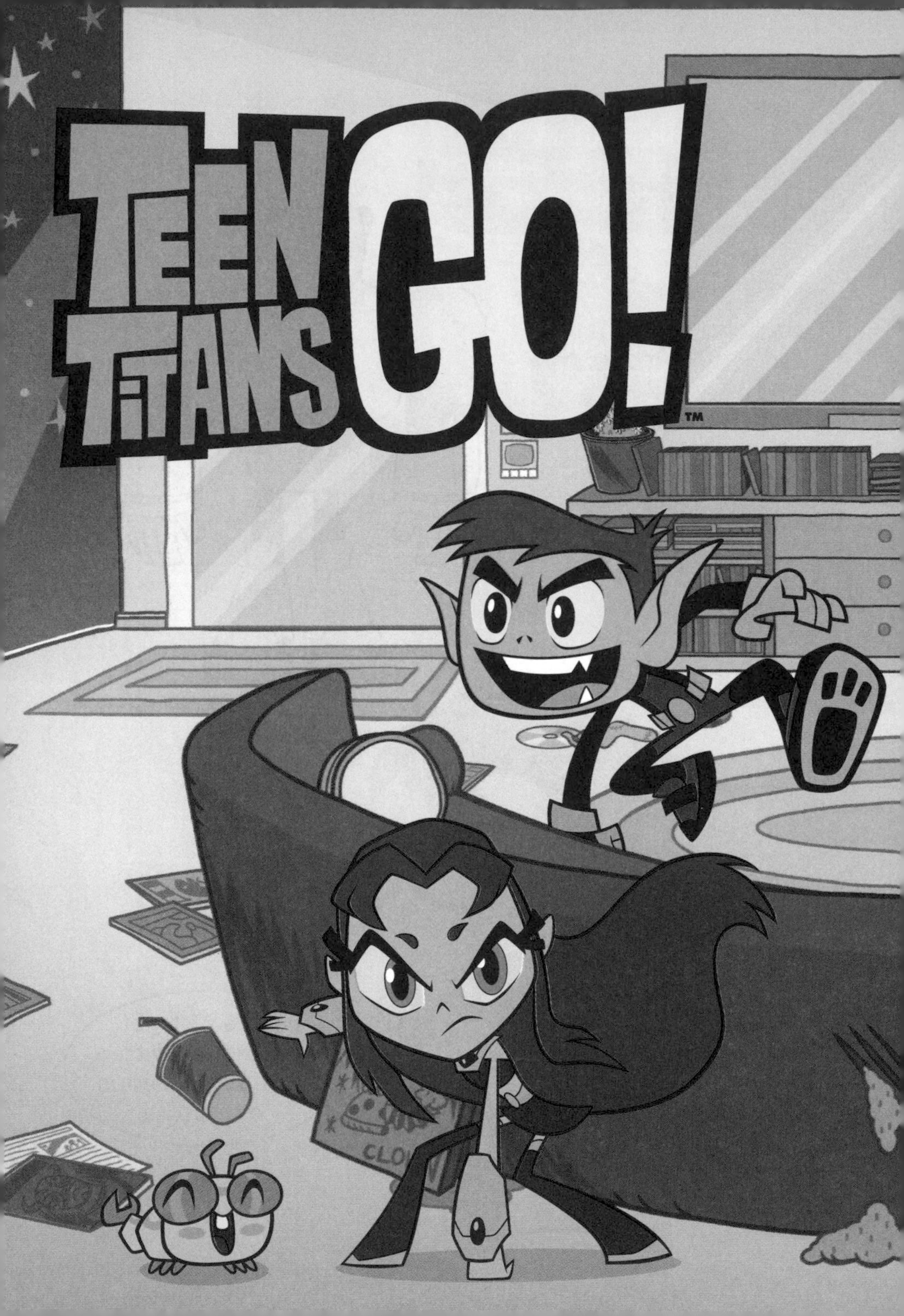
TEEN TITANS GO!™

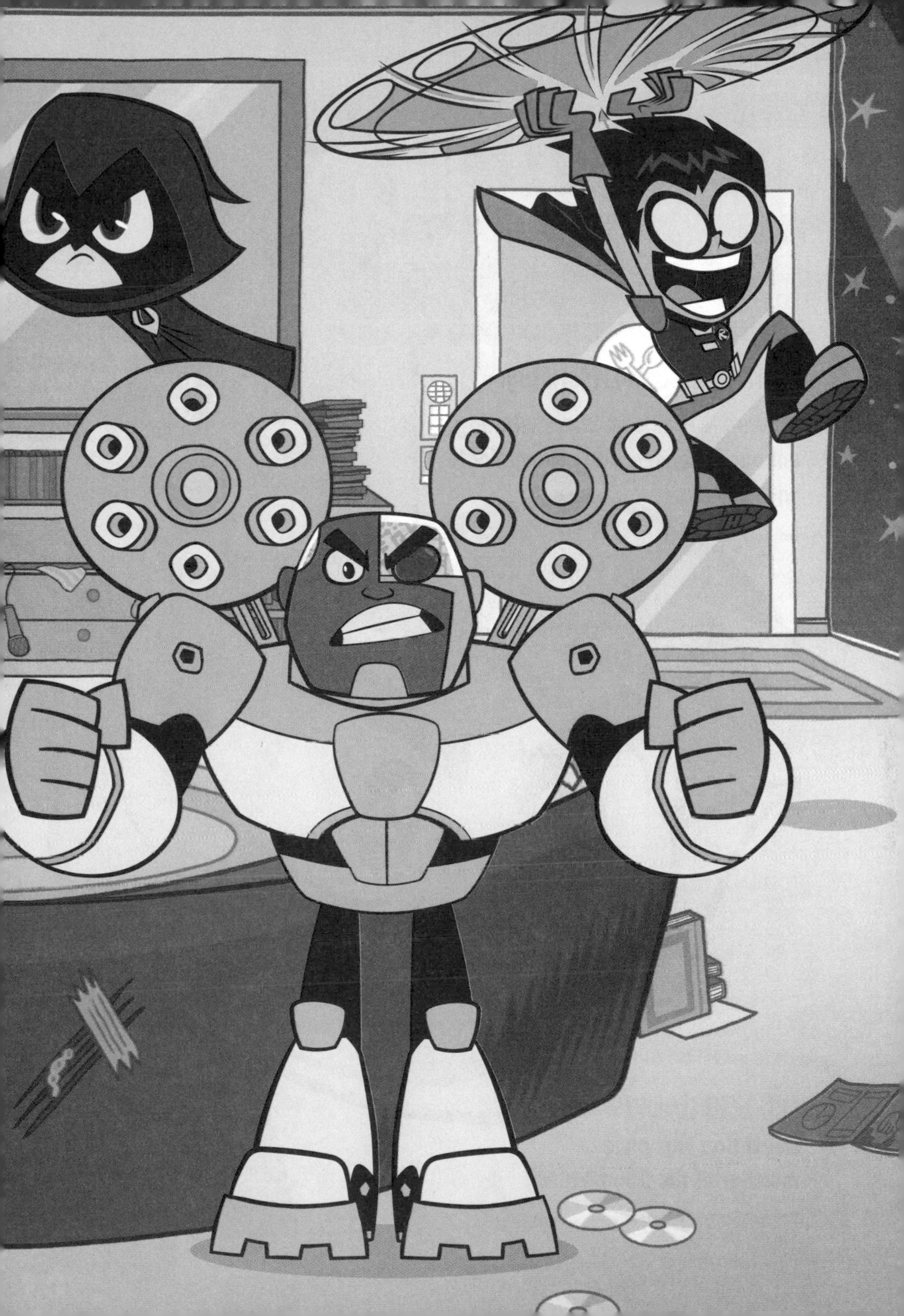

BEAST BOY

Changeling. Flirt. Bro Before Dough.

Real Name: Garfield Mark Logan

Powers & Abilities: Shape-shifting, enhanced senses, can communicate with animals

DID YOU KNOW?

Beast Boy was once a member of the Doom Patrol!

SECRET ORIGIN

My origin ain't no secret, fool! I was bitten by a radioactive monkey, got sick, turned green, got powers, became best friends with Cyborg, and joined these bozos. In that order. Oh, and I'm a vegetarian. Dat tofu iz CHOICE.

DESCRIBE YOUR PERFECT FIRST DATE....

I like to prepare a *fine* meal. As an appetizer, we got a basket of the crispiest jokes you ever heard. You feel me? After our faces are both covered in joke-crumbs, I bust out the shrimp and prime rib for her, and some shrimp-shaped tofu for me. That takes it to a whole 'nother level, bro. But that's just me. What can I say, my mode is always—

You're not really going to say it.

Eeeeee! He's gonna say it. Say it, dude. SAY IT, DUDE.

...BEAST.

And the crowd goes wild!

I can actually *hear* my eyes rolling right now.

RAVEN

Sorceress. Confidante. Demonic Diva.

Real Name: Rachel Roth

Powers & Abilities: Telekinesis, teleportation, spell-casting, can project her astral soul-self

DID YOU KNOW?
Raven's spunky catchphrase is "Azarath...Metrion... Zinthos!"

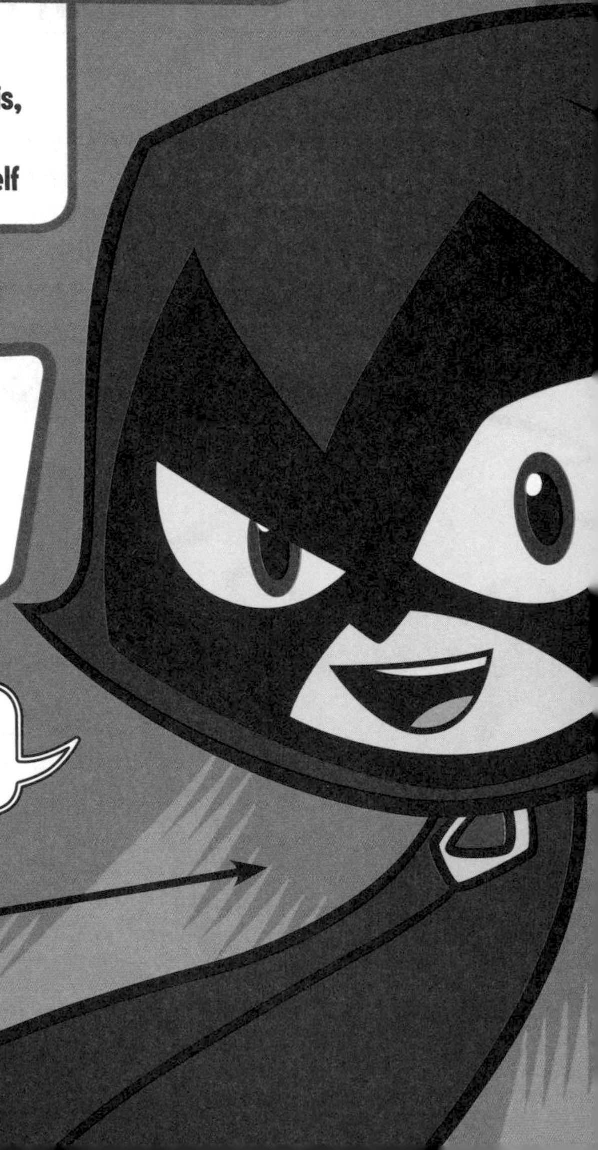
That's actually a *spell*, and it's not "spunky."
KNOW-IT-ALL

SECRET ORIGIN

Contrary to popular belief, Raven was NOT bitten by a radioactive raven. She did NOT become Raven-Woman. She did NOT lay eggs and make nests in the name of justice. She's just the daughter of a demon lord named Trigon. No biggie.

RAVEN'S DAD

Sooo, yeah, I don't know what to say here. I'm not as mysterious and dark as everyone makes me out to be. And I object to being called a "diva."

WHAT'S YOUR GUILTY PLEASURE?

Jazzercise relaxes me when the burden of existing in an unpredictable world becomes too much to bear. It's a healthy way to release my endorphins. But let's get real: It's also fun.

Shake that tush, Mama!

I am so sorry you have been burdened with so many of the endorphins, Raven. Let us ALL Jazzercise in your honor.

Thanks, Starfire.

ENDORPHINS BE GONE!

CYBORG

Man. Machine. Everything in Between.

Real Name: Vic Stone

Powers & Abilities: Super-strength, flight, has an array of cybernetic attachments (including missile launchers, rocket fists, and sonic cannons)

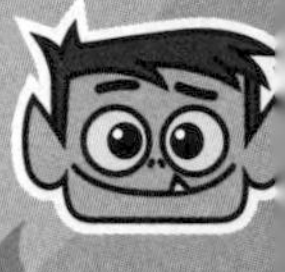

My bro of bros
Half man, half
awesome.

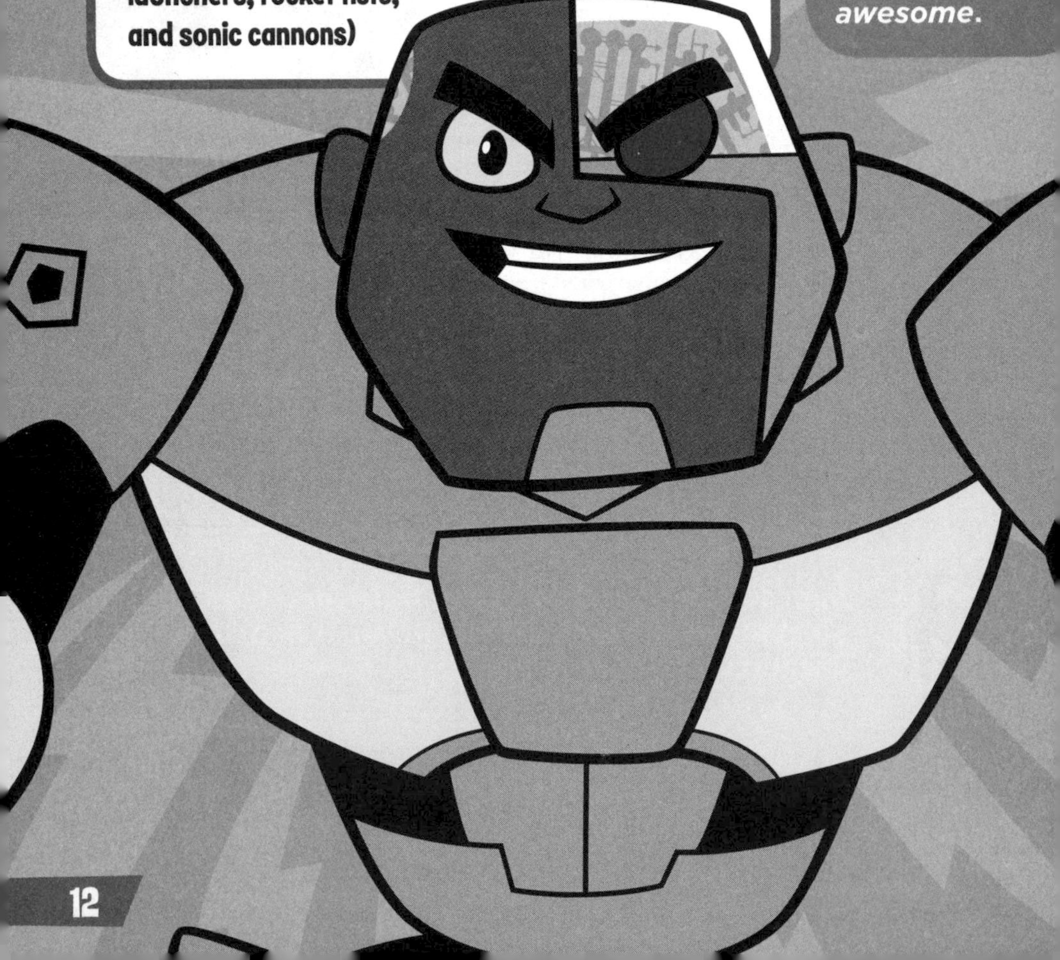

SECRET ORIGIN

Ummm, do we really have to get into my whole origin thing *right now*? I was just about to go to town on an ice cream sundae, and I don't want it to melt.

So, real quick...I started out as the best high school football star, but then something happened and I was transformed into a cyborg! I met my best friend for life, Beast Boy, and here I am. Can I go eat my ice cream now, *pleeeeeease*? Oh. You want me to do the line. *Sigh*. If I do the line, will you let me eat my ice cream?

YES

BOOYAH!

ICE CREAM UNLOCKED

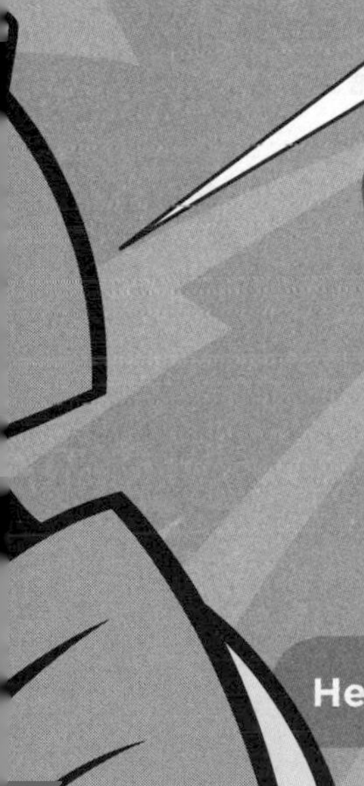

DID YOU KNOW?

Cyborg's impersonation of Lois Lane is so good he was once able to trick Superman!

DID YOU KNOW?

Cyborg's head can completely detach from his body!

Hey, why did Cyborg get *two* fun facts?

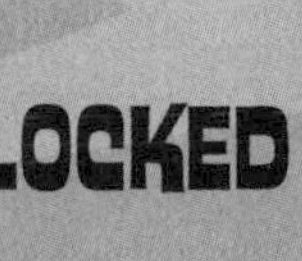

BECAUSE HE HAS A HIGHER PROFILE THAN YOU.

STARFIRE

Princess. Warrior. Kitty Kween.

Real Name: Koriand'r

Powers & Abilities: Energy projection, flight, super-strength

SECRET ORIGIN

On the distant planet of Tamaran, a young princess named Starfire dreamed of a universe where kitties and puppies lived in everlasting harmony. In order to see her vision realized, she traveled to planet Earth and joined a group of young upstart heroes known as the Teen Titans. Despite Starfire's many heroic deeds, the never-ending war between puppies and kitties rages.

One day I shall broker the peace between all warring animal groups. *One day*.

WHAT'S YOUR HIDDEN TALENT?

Talents should not be hidden! My *viewable* talent is the CRAFTING. The glitter, the glue, the hundreds of wooden Popsicle sticks!

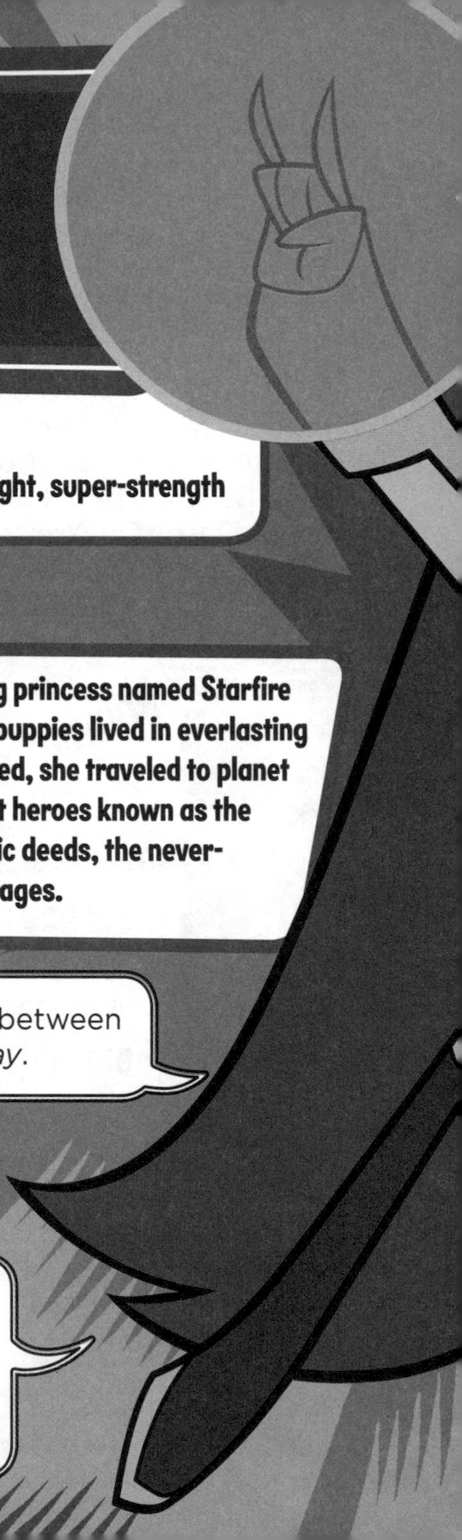

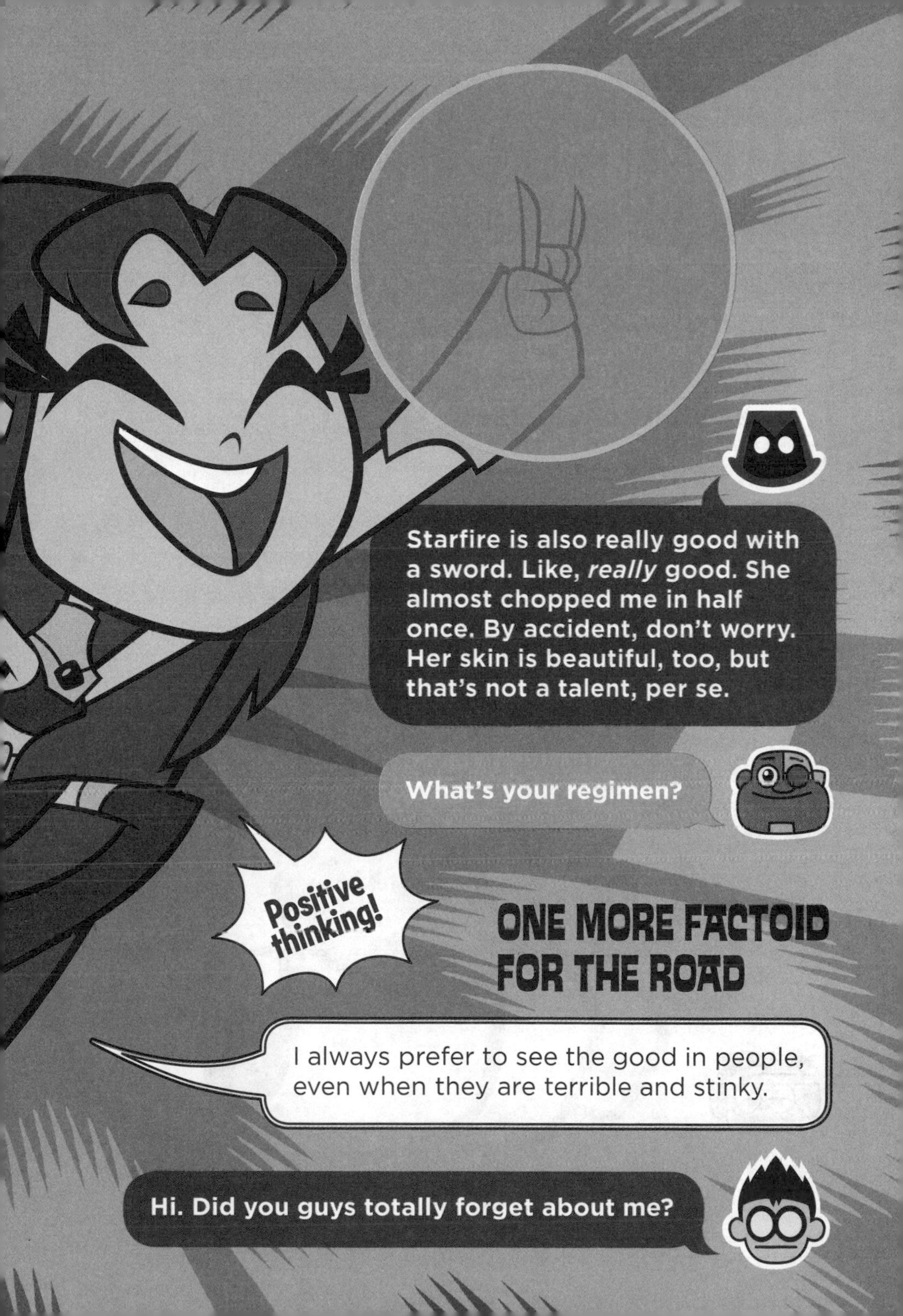
Positive thinking!

Starfire is also really good with a sword. Like, *really* good. She almost chopped me in half once. By accident, don't worry. Her skin is beautiful, too, but that's not a talent, per se.

What's your regimen?

ONE MORE FACTOID FOR THE ROAD

I always prefer to see the good in people, even when they are terrible and stinky.

Hi. Did you guys totally forget about me?

SILKIE

Soft. Sleek. Aspiring Moth.

Real Name: *Silkina T. Silkington*

Powers & Abilities: **Frequent barfer**

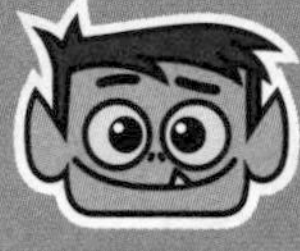

JK. I'm just playin'. Silkie is just Silkie.

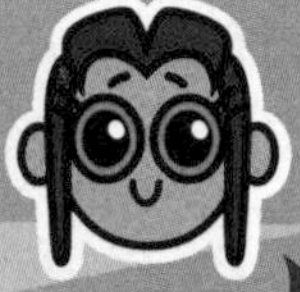

Dearest Silkie, you are the prettiest mutant moth larva I've ever been gifted!

You make me the happy. It was the destiny that Beast Boy liberated you from the clutches of Killer Moth and brought you into my life, dear friend.

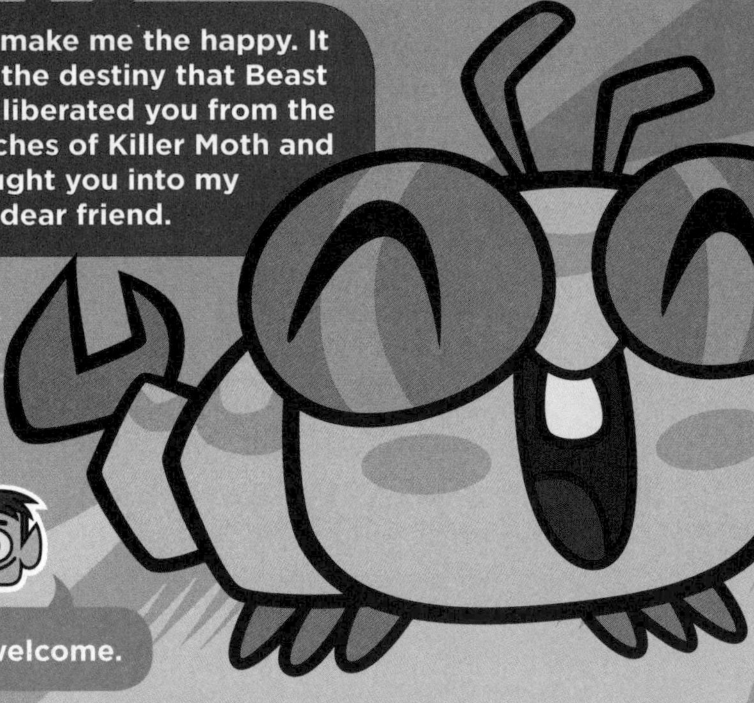

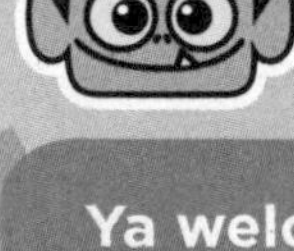

Ya welcome.

SILKIEBOT

Mega Metal Silkie

And look at the beautiful world-saving armor you built all by yourself, Silkie. What a treasure your brilliance is. We are the grateful.

Silkiebot got a mention before me? Huh. Okay. I see you, Silkiebot. I see who you are.

However, according to my keen sense of fairness, my profile should be coming...

up... next....

KID FLASH

Really Fast. Really Annoying.

Real Name: Wally West

Powers & Abilities: Super-speed, can vibrate through stuff, limited time travel

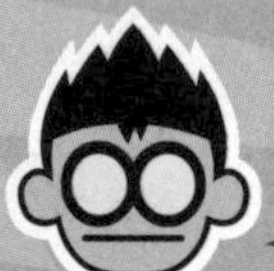

WHAT?! How did Kid Flash get in here? He's not even a full-time member.

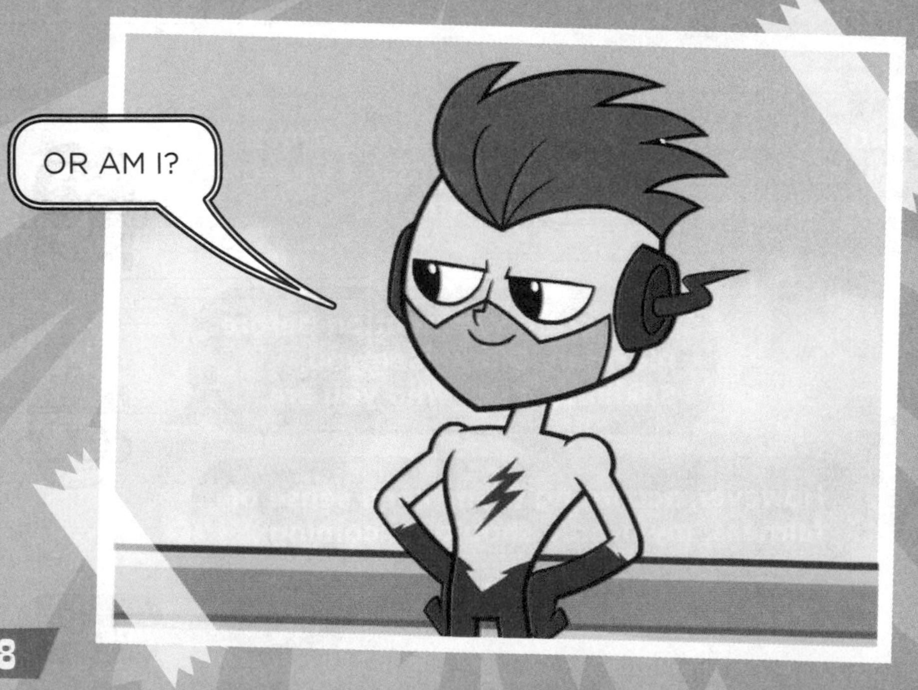
OR AM I?

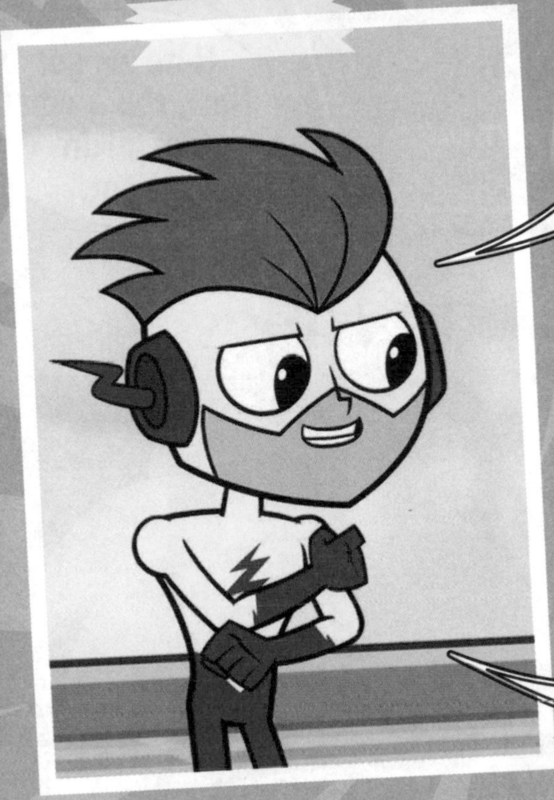

SECRET ORIGIN

It's too much to get into. Don't worry about it.

This is a sham!

Chill, man. Relax and accept the glory of Kid Flash.

We get zero details on this guy's backstory, and yet he still gets a profile before I do?!

Grrrrrrrr.

And talking in third person is *ROBIN'S* THING.

ROBIN

Sidekick. Acrobat. Future Nightwing.

Real Name: Dick Grayson

Powers & Abilities: Master detective, hand-to-hand combat, acrobatics, agility, ability to hide tiny hands in normal-size gloves

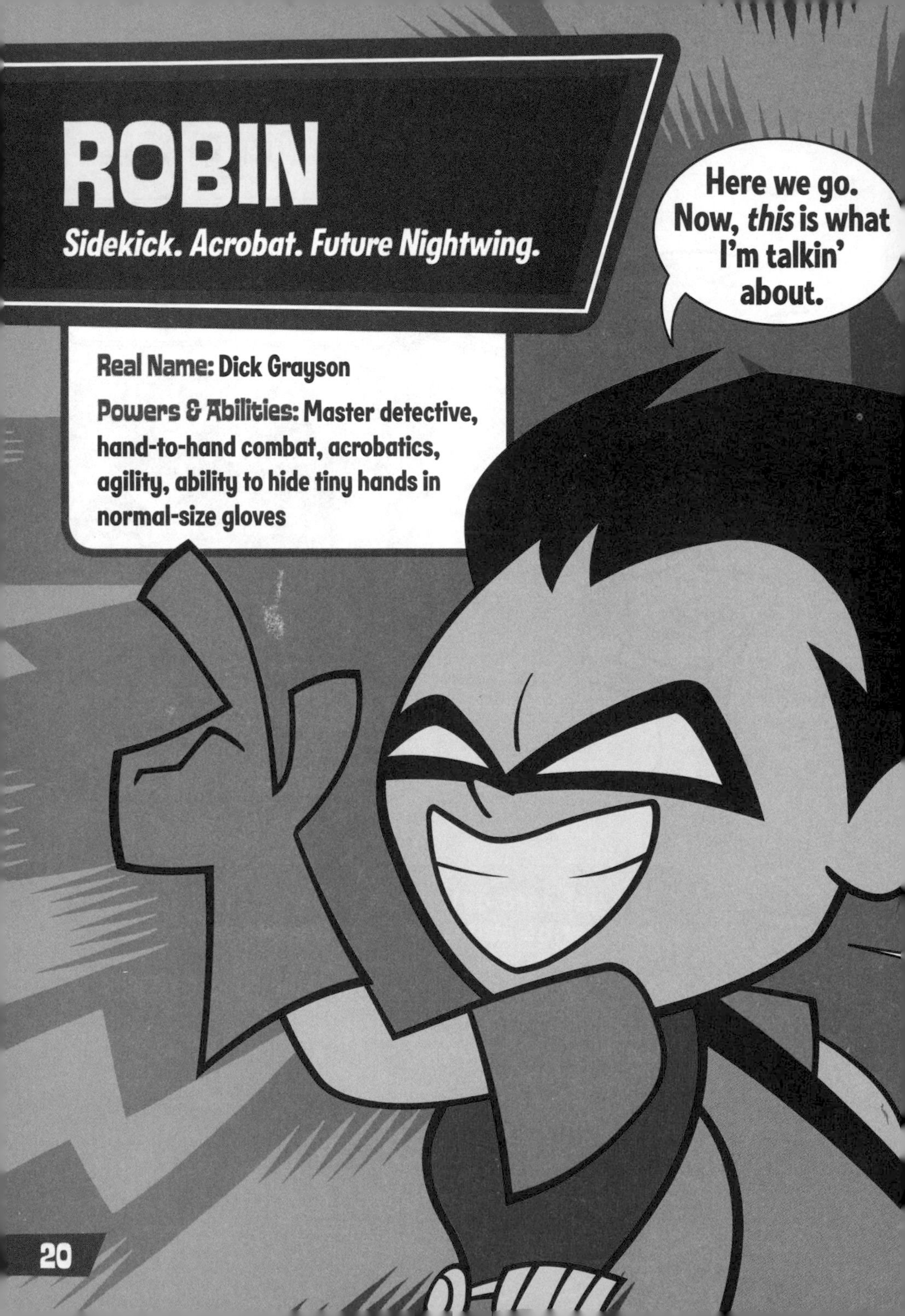
Here we go. Now, *this* is what I'm talkin' about.

SECRET ORIGIN

It was a dark and smelly afternoon. I was having a taco-eating contest with myself. Raven was in the bathroom casting an evil spell on the toilet.

Cyborg was fighting Pie Hunter in cyberspace. Starfire was braiding Silkie's antennae. Then, like a gift from the heavens, a sweet li'l nugget of a boy walked into our lives, changing us forever.

Be serious, Beast Boy.

I *am* serious, bro. You're a sweet li'l nugget who changed us forever.

I meant, that's *not* my secret origin.

But, Robin, that's the thing—*what if it is*?!

It's not!

GRRR. BEAST BOY, YOU JUST WASTED SO MUCH TIME ON A BUNCH OF NONSENSE!

You just need to believe in yourself.

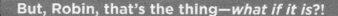

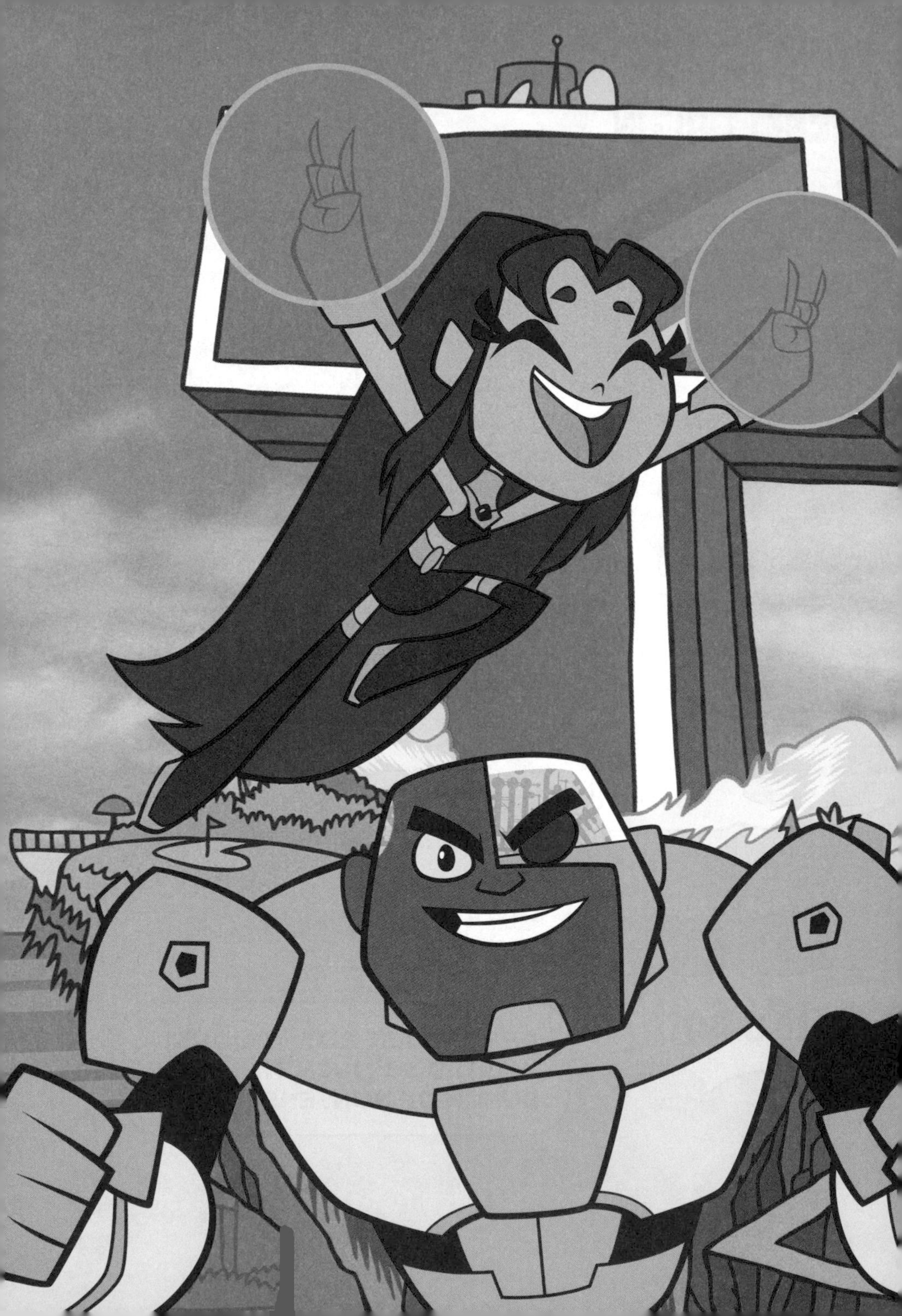

LOCATIONS AND GADGETS

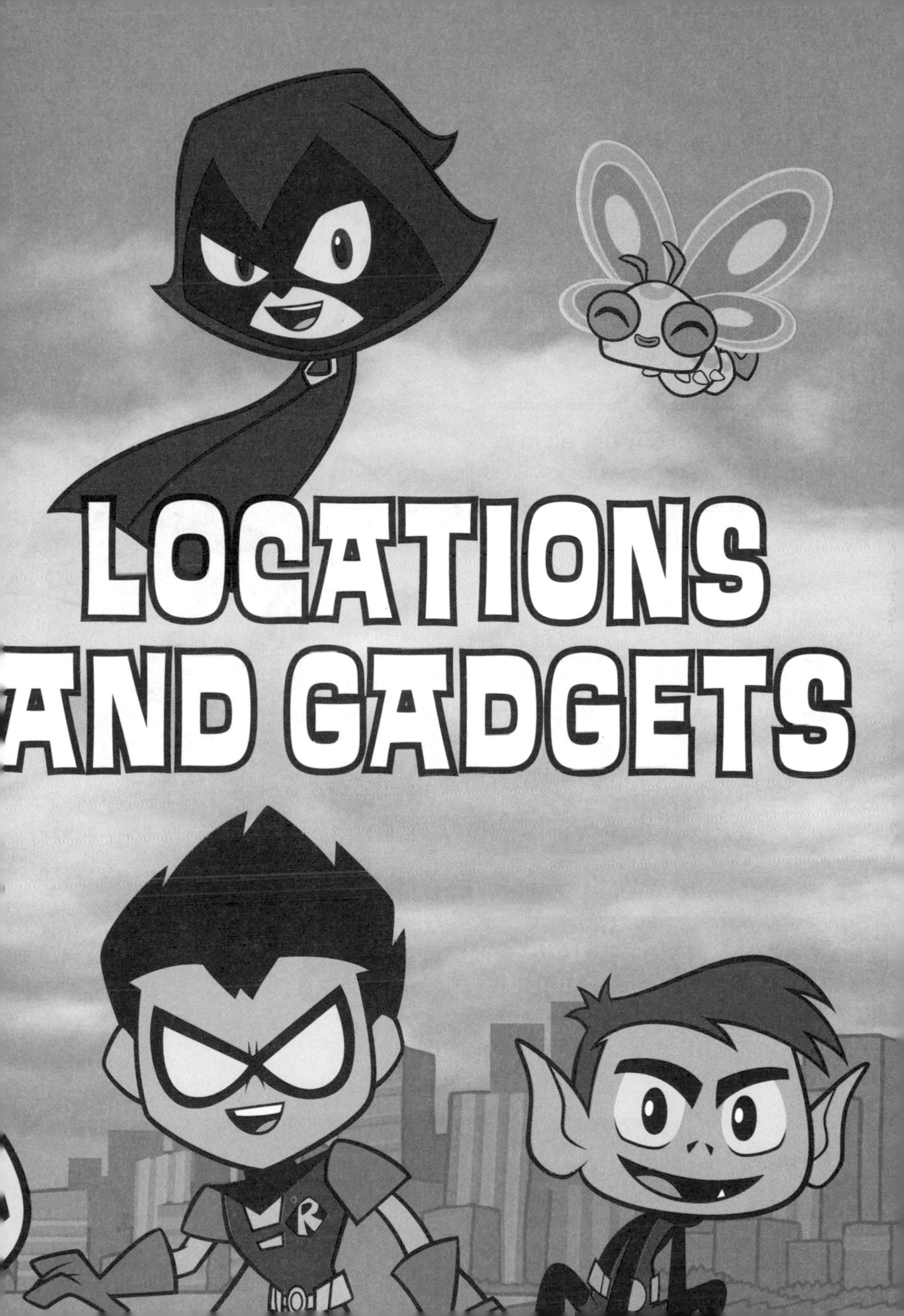

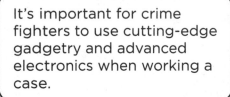

It's important for crime fighters to use cutting-edge gadgetry and advanced electronics when working a case.

Good heroes must always be ahead of the curve.

Hey, *Raven*. I gots some cutting-edge gadgetry around here, too! I just needs to find it in all this junk.

Sorry, Beast Boy. It doesn't count if you can't find it.

Hurray for the organizational skills!

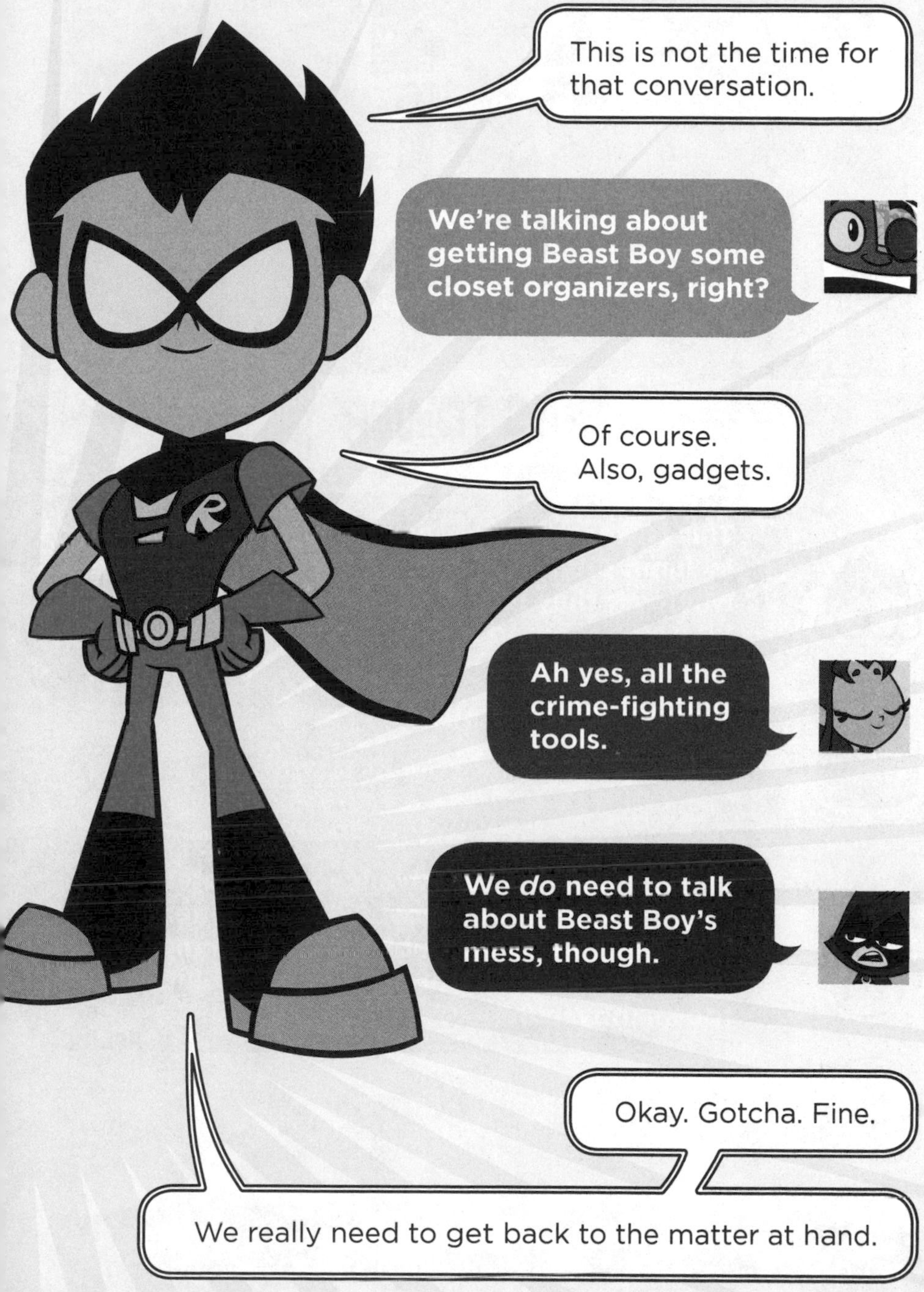
This is not the time for that conversation.
We're talking about getting Beast Boy some closet organizers, right?
Of course. Also, gadgets.
Ah yes, all the crime-fighting tools.
We *do* need to talk about Beast Boy's mess, though.
Okay. Gotcha. Fine.
We really need to get back to the matter at hand.

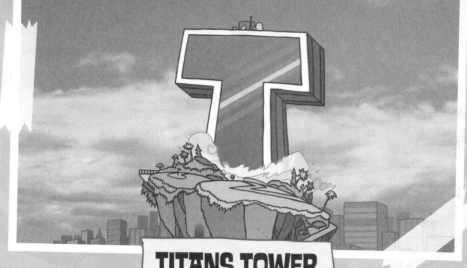

TITANS TOWER

This is where it all goes down. From our hub in Jump City, the Titans can monitor evildoers wherever they might be hiding. We won't rest till we've scoured every dark underbelly looking for vile scum.

Ewwwwwww. That sounds disgusting.

Titans Tower has an advanced computer filled with data on all our most villainous enemies. *And* we've got a state-of-the-art training facility where we sharpen our powers and abilities. Not too shabby, huh?

WE HAVE A TRAINING FACILITY?

Yeah, bro. And there's a washing machine in the basement cuz all y'all STANK.

Even though our aircraft is not invisible like the Wonder Woman's, this does not mean it isn't worthy of the love. The T-Plane also comes with parachutes.

T-PLANE

Parachutes! How exciting!

Sure, if we're about to crash, they're awesome.

TITAN ROBOT

My sweet baby. I built the Titan Robot for those special times when we need to show a bad guy he's in over his head.

Each section is controlled by a different team member, and if we want to kick up the firepower, we've got to work together. It's not as easy as it sounds.

What dance does a robot do in a dance-off?

THE HUMAN.

Now, *this* is a ride. The branding is *on point*.

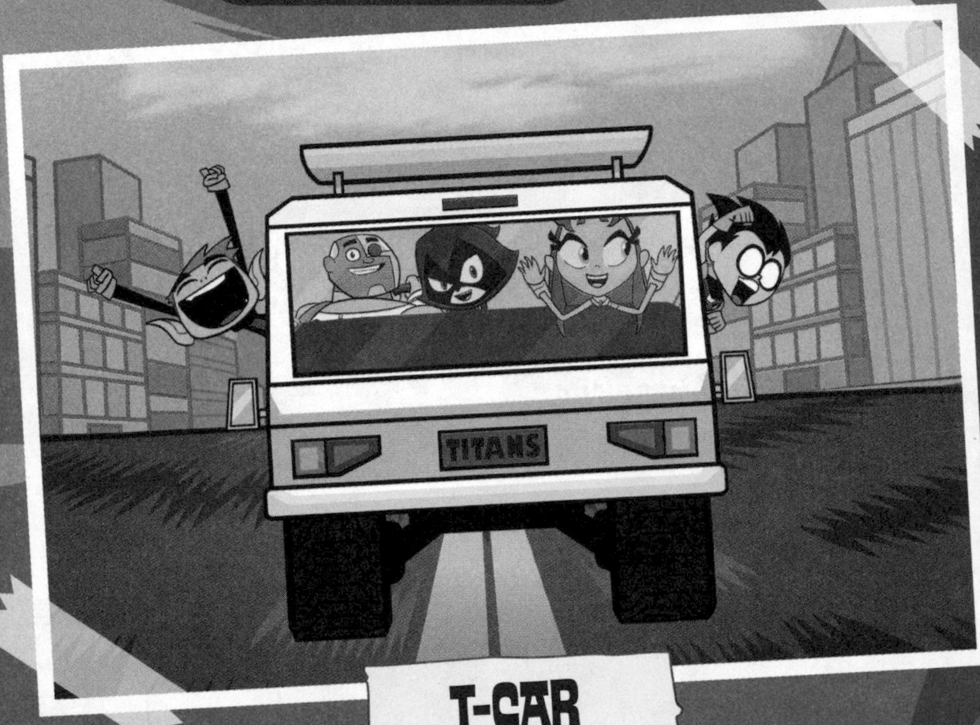
TITANS

T-CAR

Not to mention all the bells and whistles we can't see like the rocket boosters, turret cannon, GPS tracking, Italian leather seats, and sizable cup holders for maximum drink safety.

And you can drive it!

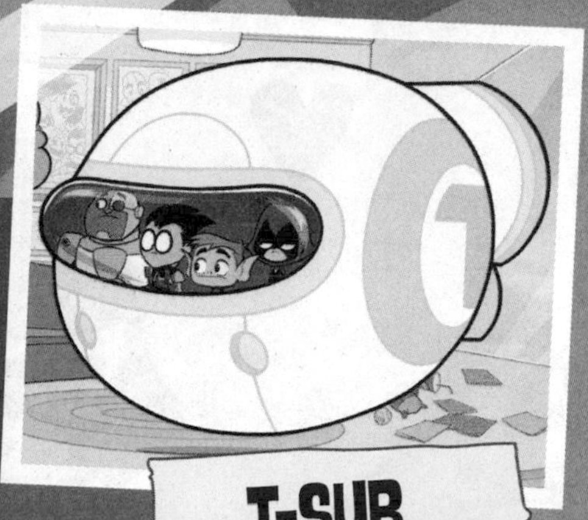

The depths of the ocean can be the scary. I am grateful to have an air-conditioned safe place where sharks cannot find me and eat me.

T-SUB

Yeah, it's cozy. The T-Sub can also shrink down to microscopic size and enter your body, so that's fun. I bet you wish I'd never told you that.

Luxury!

Decadence! A working hot tub!

TITAN YACHT

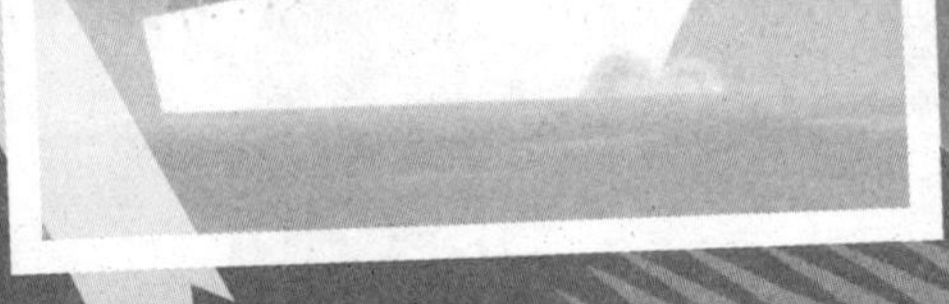

The Titan Yacht is a dream come true (until you realize that it takes a lot of time and energy to clean a big ol' boat).

Yer killin' me, yo. Throw some mad-fun parties and don't worry about it. In the Titan Yacht, T-Car, switchin' four lanes with the top down, screaming out, "Burritos ain't a thang!"

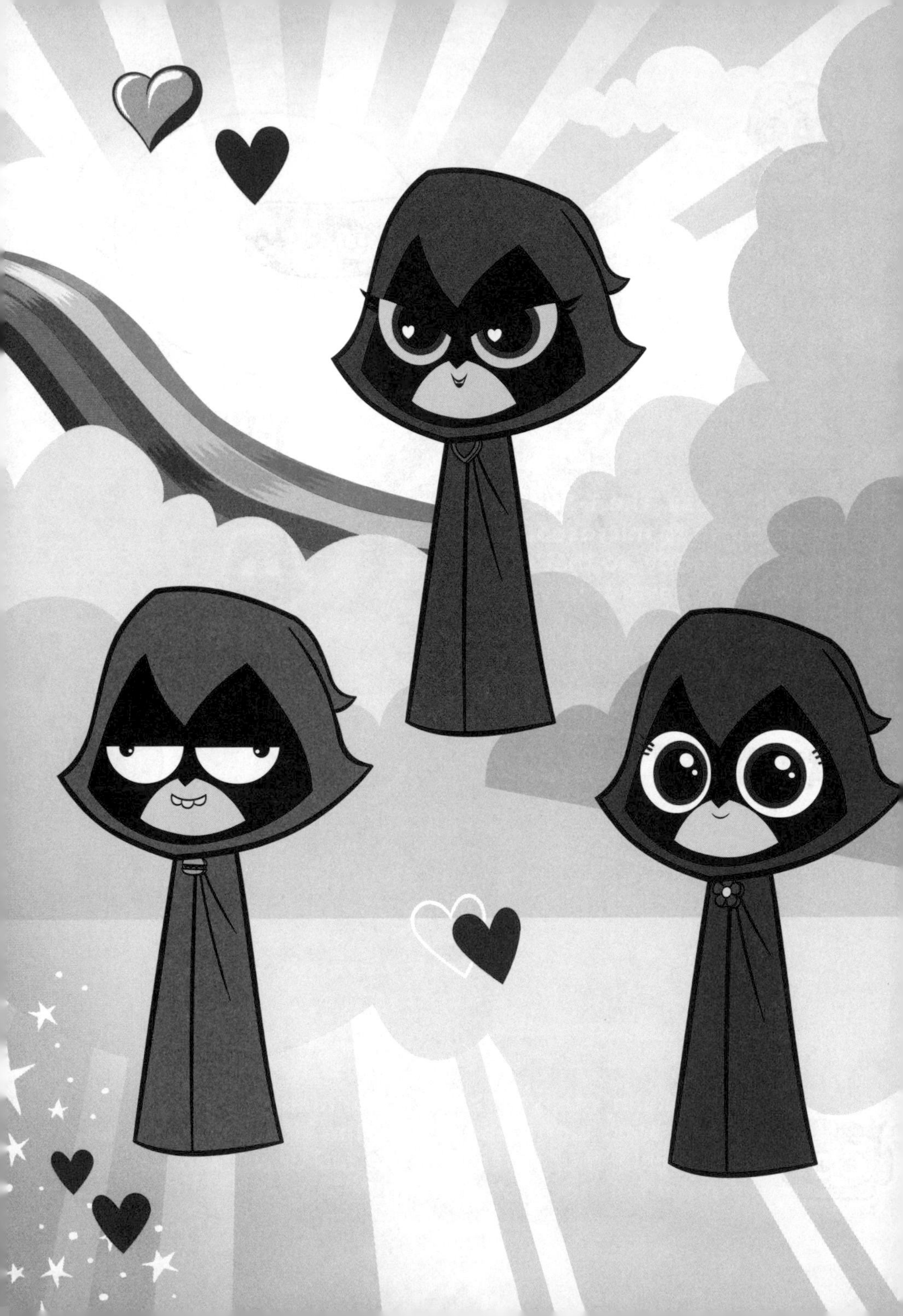

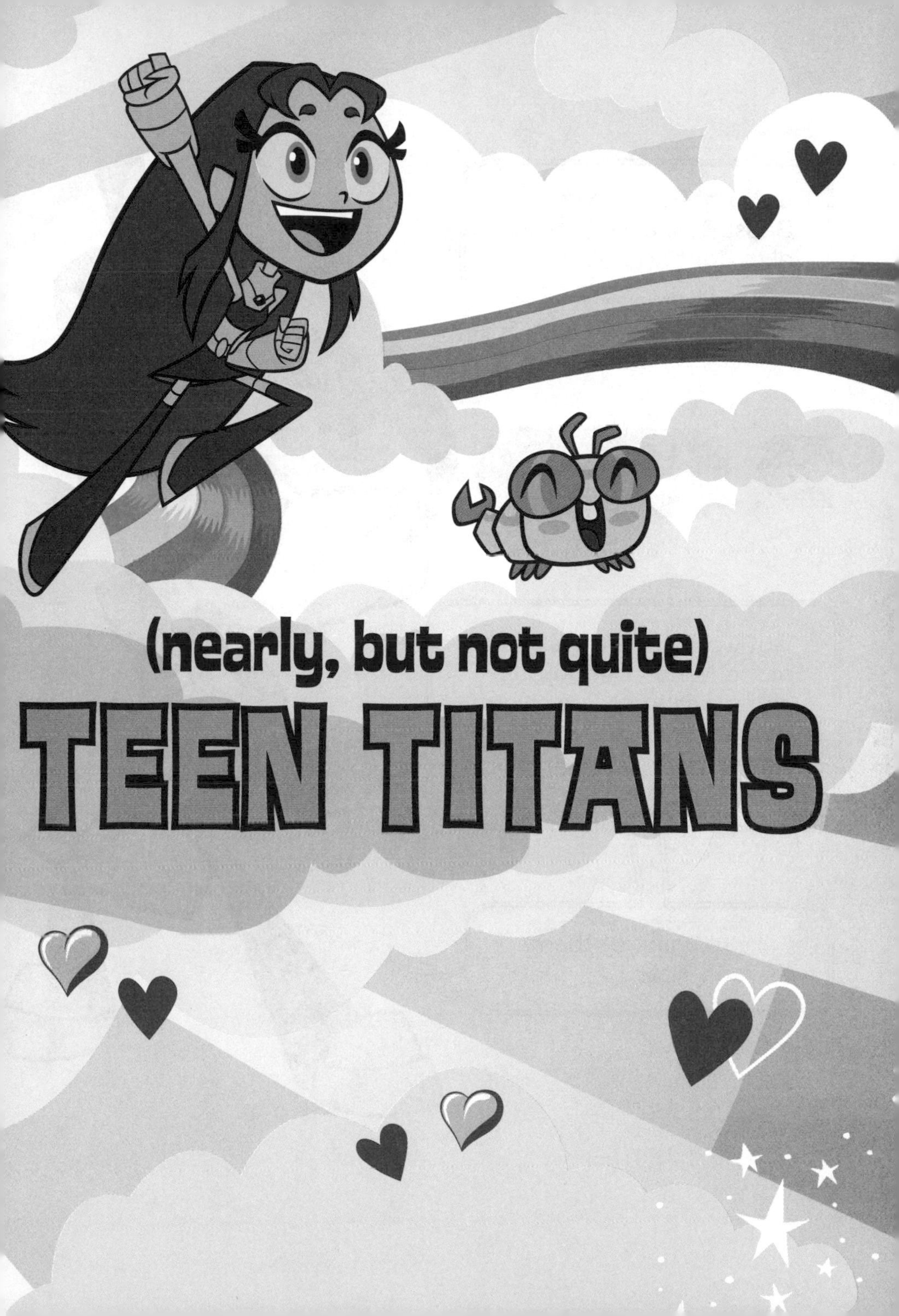
(nearly, but not quite)
TEEN TITANS

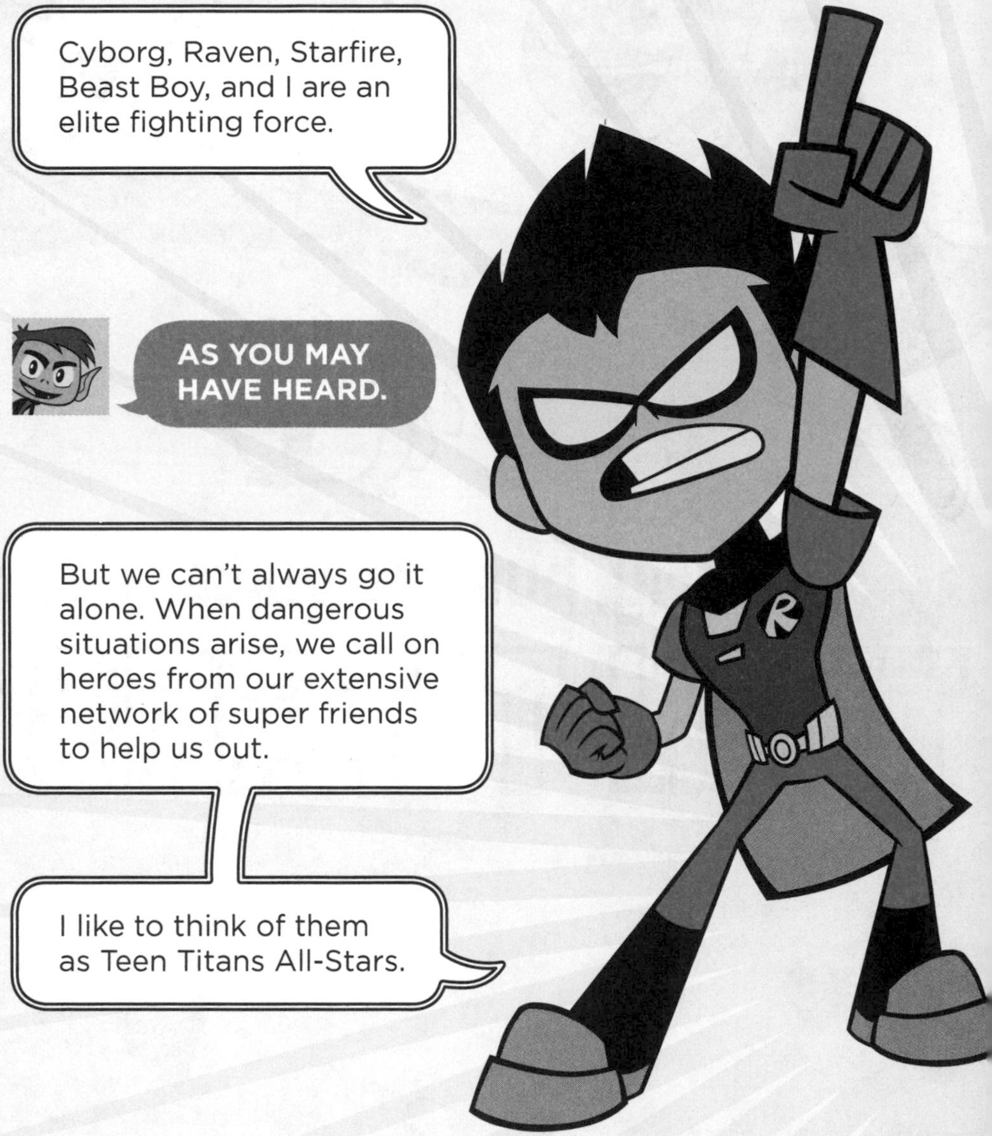
Cyborg, Raven, Starfire, Beast Boy, and I are an elite fighting force.
AS YOU MAY HAVE HEARD.
But we can't always go it alone. When dangerous situations arise, we call on heroes from our extensive network of super friends to help us out.
I like to think of them as Teen Titans All-Stars.

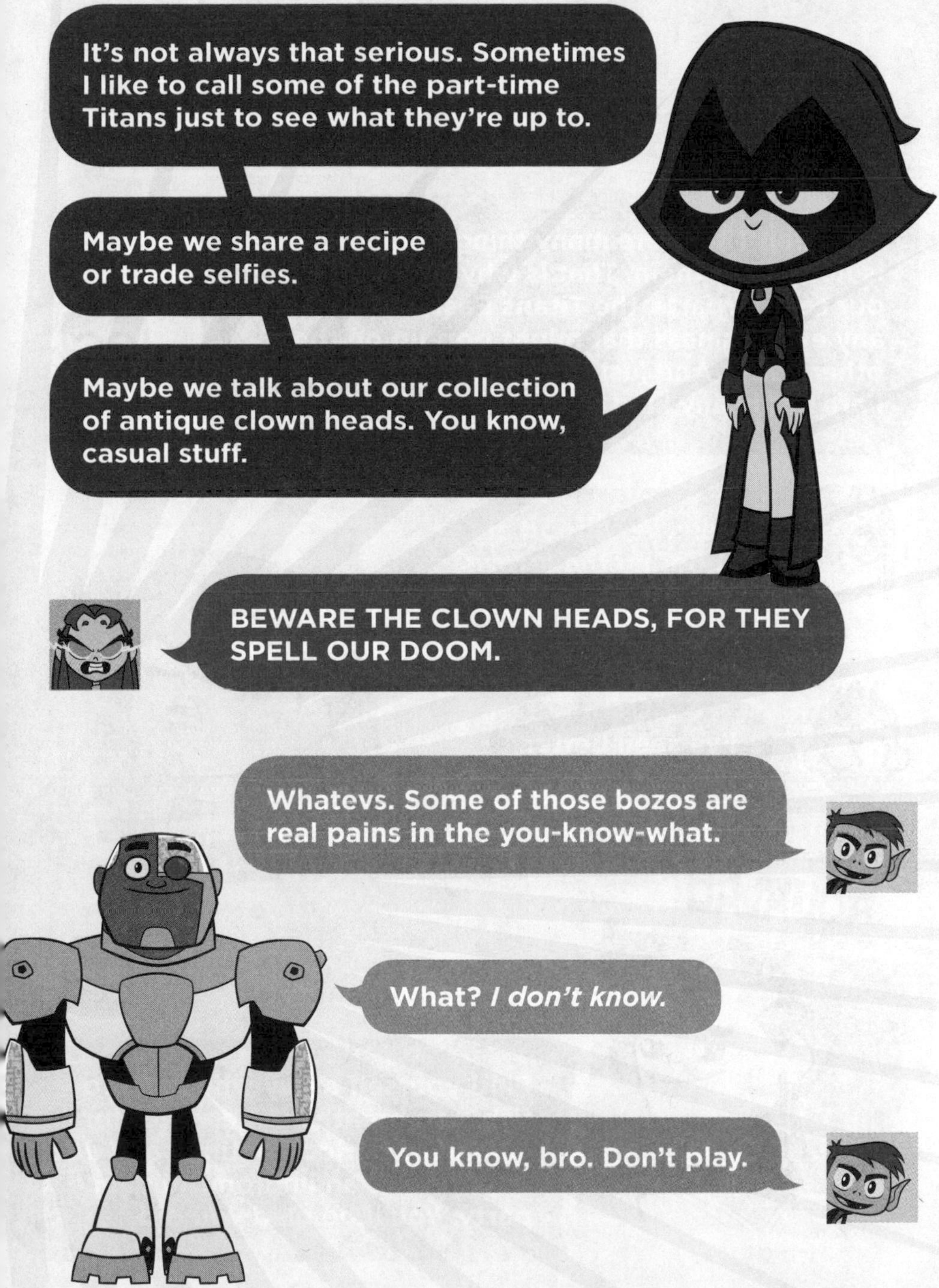

It's not always that serious. Sometimes I like to call some of the part-time Titans just to see what they're up to.
Maybe we share a recipe or trade selfies.
Maybe we talk about our collection of antique clown heads. You know, casual stuff.
BEWARE THE CLOWN HEADS, FOR THEY SPELL OUR DOOM.
Whatevs. Some of those bozos are real pains in the you-know-what.
What? *I don't know.*
You know, bro. Don't play.

TITANS EAST

The Teen Titans are many things, but *bicoastal* is not one of them. That is why we rely on our counterparts, the Titans East, to handle any evil business that might pop up on the other coast. And just to be clear, Speedy and I are not in any kind of competition.

He is very good at shooting the arrows. So steady, so focused, so strong.

I've seen better.

SPEEDY

AQUALAD

Find yourself a guy who talks to fish, can breathe underwater for extended periods of time, and *also* appreciates an impromptu dance party. You'll be glad you did.

BUMBLEBEE

One time I thought Bumblebee was a real bee and almost swatted her. I didn't! But I almost did. She stung me anyway, but I kind of deserved it.

Bro, she buzzin'!

MÁS Y MENOS

These identical twin brothers have super-speed abilities, but only when they're able to physically touch each other. Plus, they make a tasty tamale. Did I cover everything?

More or less.

LITTLE BUDDIES

Pets. Sidekicks. Confidants. The Little Buddies are always there for us. Through thick and thin! Our relationship with them wasn't so great at first, but when you're dealing with animals, unpredictable robots, and li'l devils, you learn to roll with the punches.

BIRDARANG

Microchips + my favorite Birdarang = the best talking weapon a crime fighter could ask for.

BEAT BOX

Who knew that stabbing a Beat Box in the heart would make it magically come alive? I'm actually still processing the whole thing.

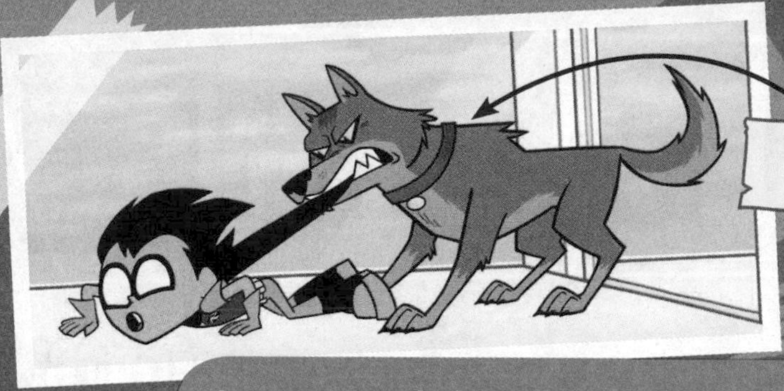

DAVE

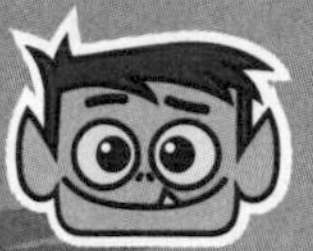

Awww. My wittle salivating, territorial wolfie. Don't bite Wobin, *mmmkay*?

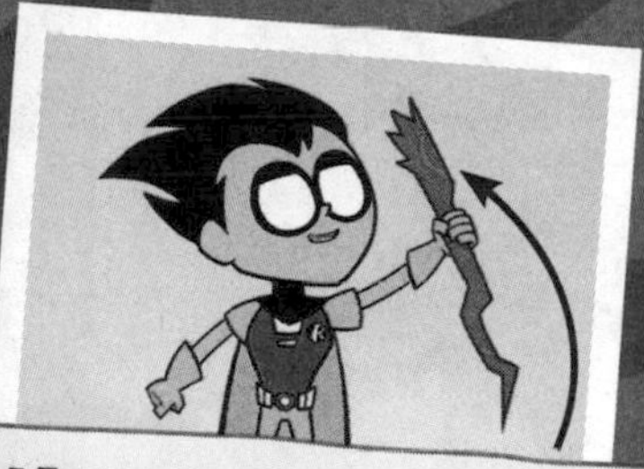

UNIVERSE STAFF

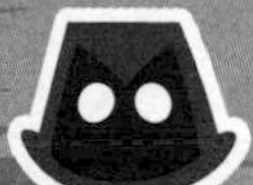

He's in charge of all the—DRAMATIC SIGH—*staff meetings*. (Who writes this stuff?)

PAIN BOT

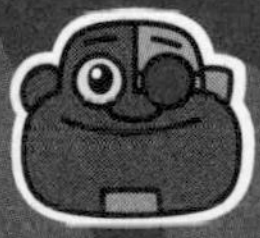

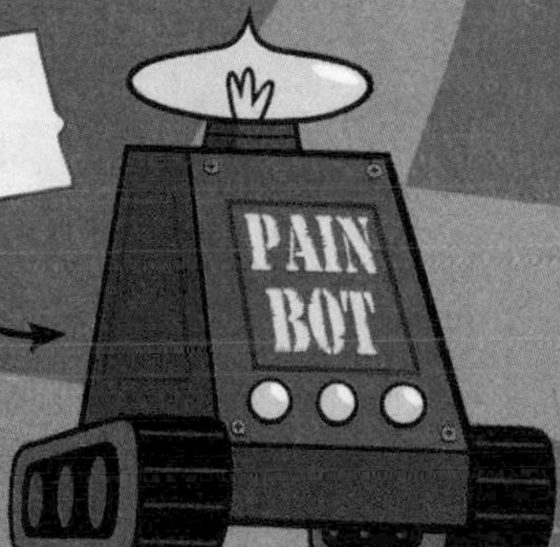
PAIN
BOT

Brother Blood built him to inflict pain and suffering. Then I showed him love. Nothing was the same again.

DEMON

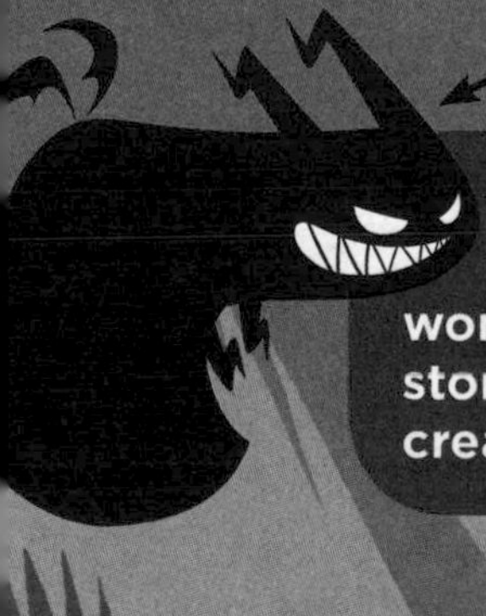

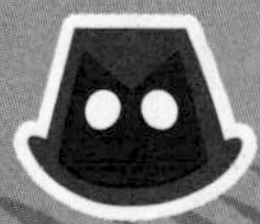

I tried banishing Demon to another dimension, and now he won't leave me alone. It'd be a sweet story if he wasn't a soul-gobbling creature of darkness.

BIZARRO TITANS

GROBYC!

ERIFRATS!

NEVAR!

NIBOR!

BOY BEAST!

It's good to see our Bizarro World pals again. They really understand me as a person. All of them except Nibor. That guy's a real idiot. Kidding! They're all great. (Not really.)

EMOTICLONES

If you ever find a Mysterious Prism that has the power to split you and your friends into emotionally charged copies of yourselves, don't touch it.

Jus' sayin'.

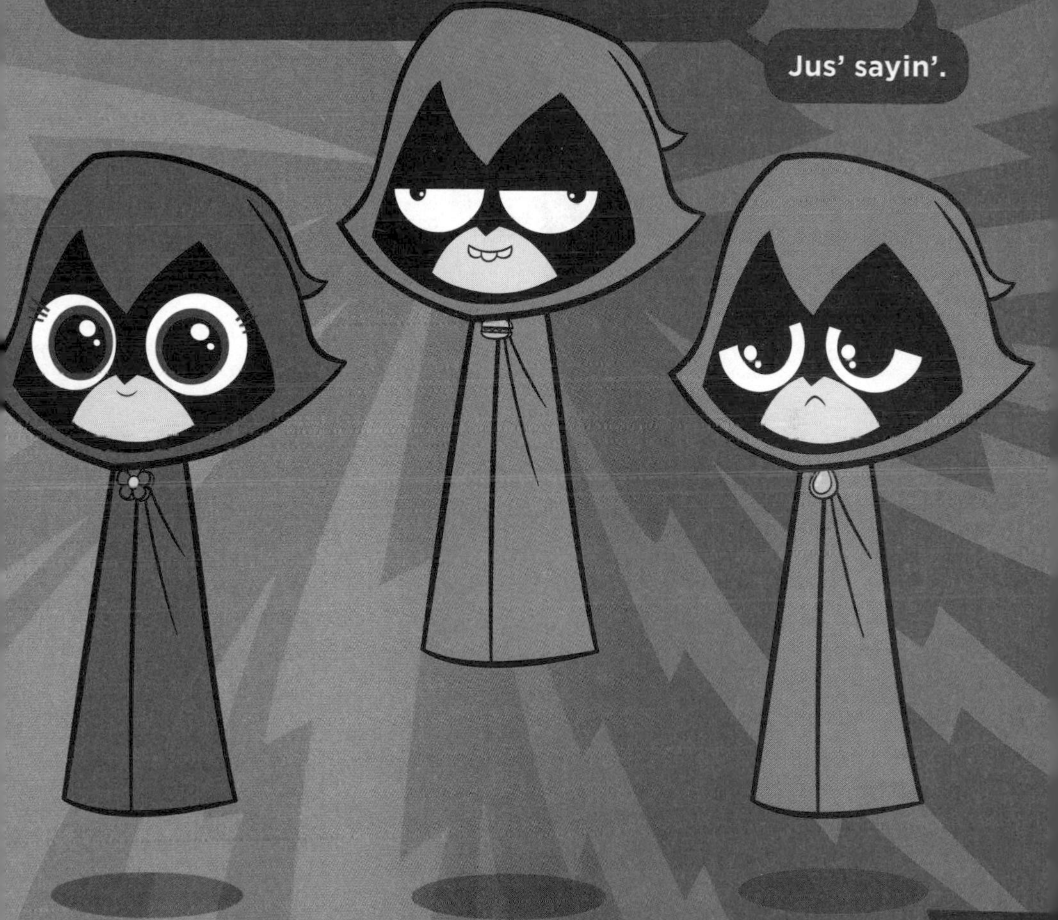

LEAGUE OF LEGS

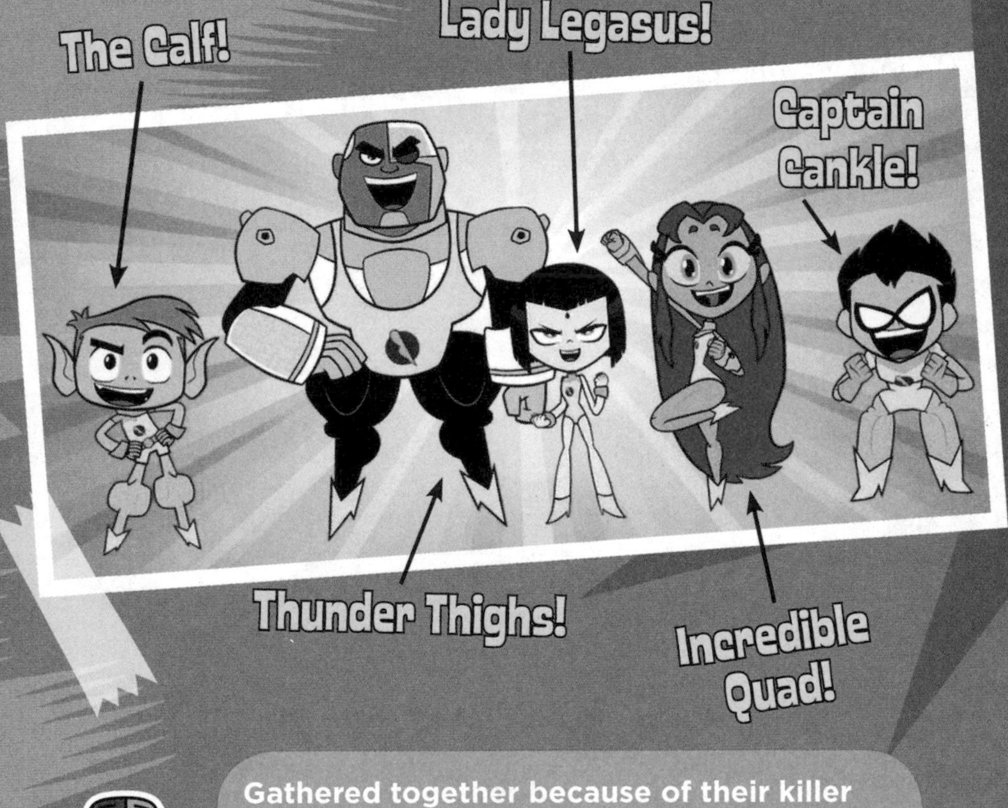
The Calf!
Lady Legasus!
Captain Cankle!
Thunder Thighs!
Incredible Quad!

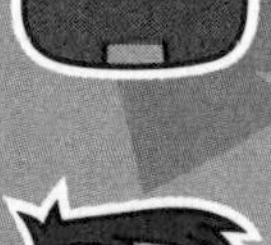

Gathered together because of their killer getaway sticks, in a tower that's shaped like a leg, these are five of the most gam-tacular super heroes ever assembled.

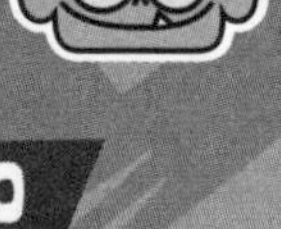

Because *every* day is Leg Day.

LEGION OF *DOOOOM*

Dick Gravestone!

The Cyborg!

Beast Monster!

Demon of Azarath!

Starfire the Terrible!

Everyone has a smidgen of the darkness inside them, even the Teen Titans.

People do not think *I* am capable of making the evil, because I have chosen a path of kindness and understanding, BUT I AM.

She's not kidding.

YOUNG JUSTICE

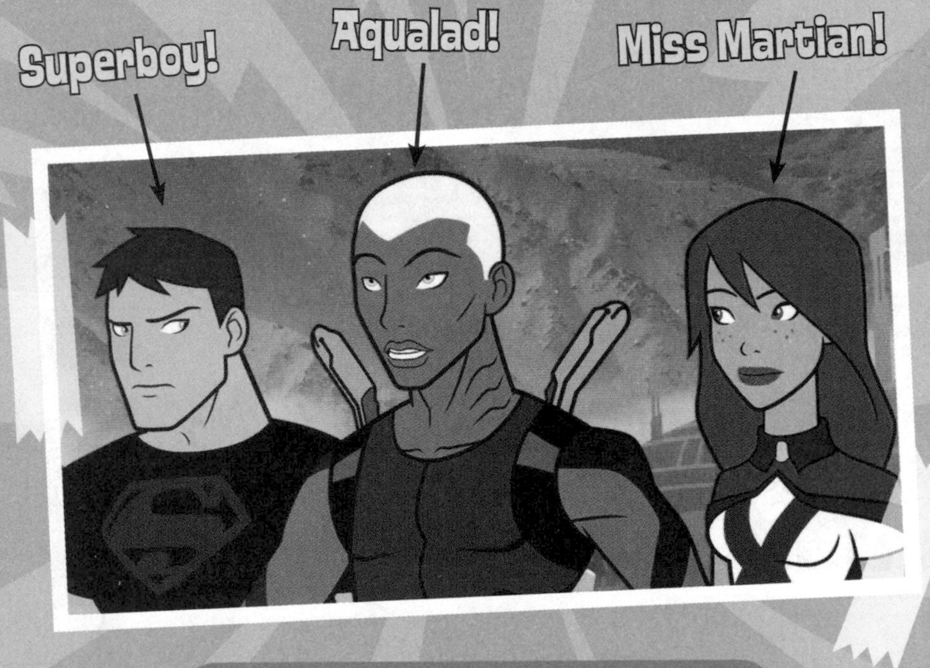
Superboy!
Aqualad!
Miss Martian!

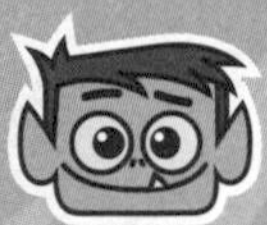

These dudes are way too serious, yo.

It's like they're from another universe. But dat Miss Martian can hit me up anytime she wants. Gotta support a fellow greenie.

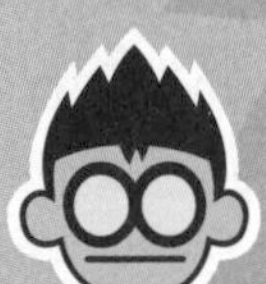

Superboy and Aqualad are far too hunky for combat. It's distracting.

NIGHTWING

One day I'm going to rise from boy wonder-hood and become a dark avenger of the night. *This* is my destiny. No one will ever be able to change that.

Nice hair, yo.

It is like the mane of a most beautiful steed!

Mullet-tastic.

This is the darkest future I've ever seen.

TEAM ROBIN

Huzzah!

Now we're talkin'.

My SKWAD!

SILVER AGE ROBIN!

Don't say SKWAD, bro. No one calls it that.

TIM DRAKE!

This is a *team*. Forged in the fires of sidekickdom, Team Robin stands against all forms of villainy. Hear our cry—

CAW, CAW!

CAW, CAW!

You missed a few.

What? No, I didn't.

Yes, you did.

CARRIE KELLEY!

What about Stephanie Brown? What about Duke Thomas? What about Damian Wayne? Not to mention all the Elseworlds Robins.

I don't...Wait...Who are those people?

SUPER ROBIN!

ROBINS.

Not ringing any bells. Sorry.

I should really build an army of Cyborgs one of these days.

Been there, done that.

45

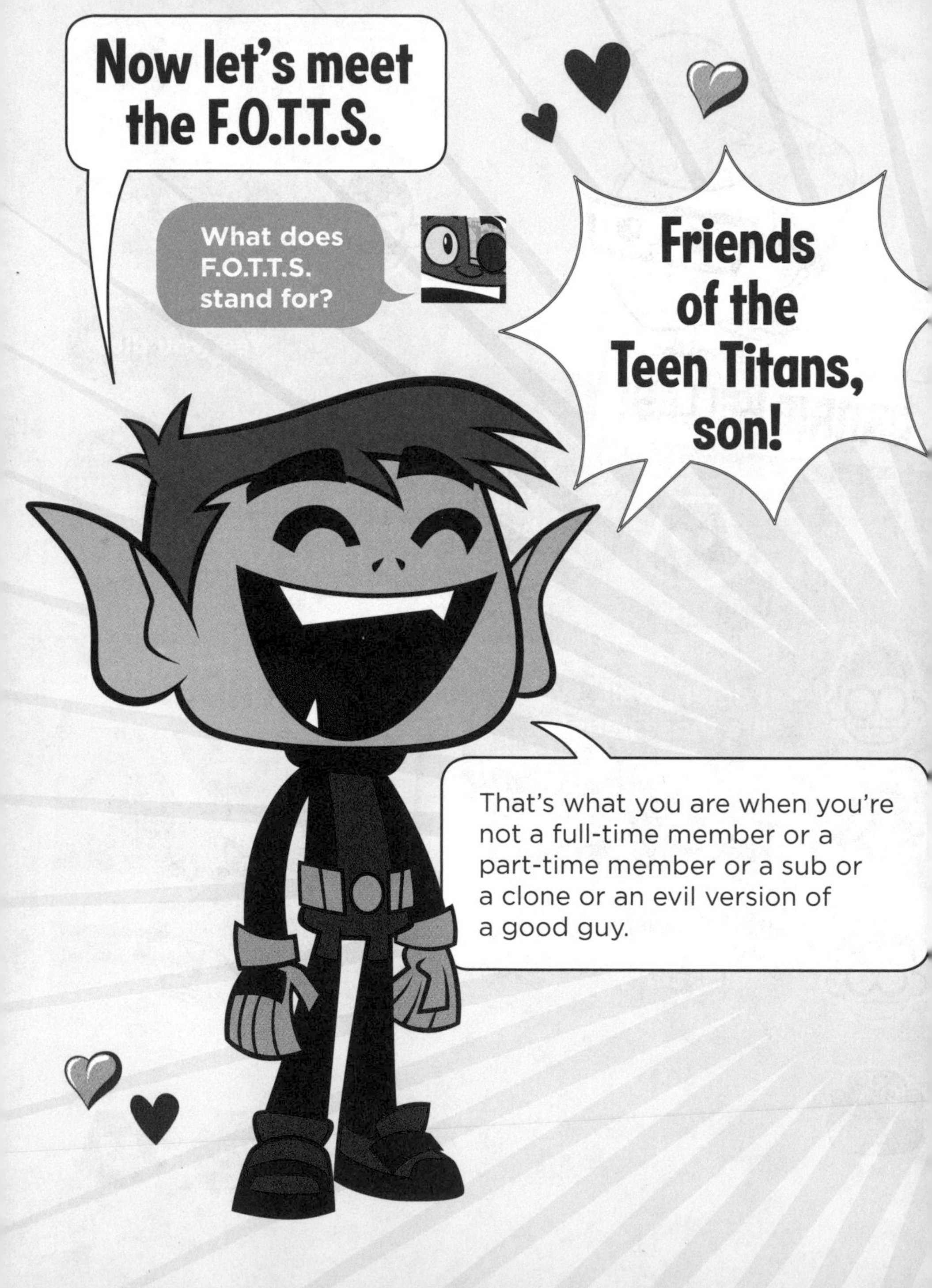
Now let's meet the F.O.T.T.S.
What does F.O.T.T.S. stand for?
Friends of the Teen Titans, son!
That's what you are when you're not a full-time member or a part-time member or a sub or a clone or an evil version of a good guy.

Friends are just like family except they are not related to you by blood. Friends are the chosen.

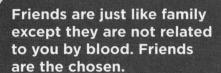 F.O.T.T.S. is kind of an offensive term, guys.

These days we call them Titan Adjacents.

They're just super heroes, guys.

We don't need to brand everything for our own needs.

HAVE YOU *MET* US?

THE WONDER TWINS

Turning into water and animals when you fist-bump?

Okay, I feel you. But these fools need some spice. How about a friendly helper monkey?

Gleek, gleek!

Or a new outfit. They look like an alien circus act.

Called it.

We *are* an alien circus act.

ZAN

JAYNA

VIXEN

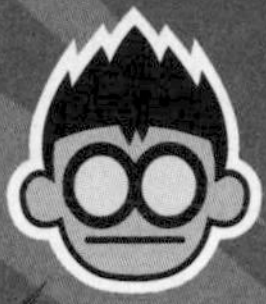

Vixen is a force to be reckoned with. Using her mystical Tantu Totem, she can command the full power of the animal kingdom.

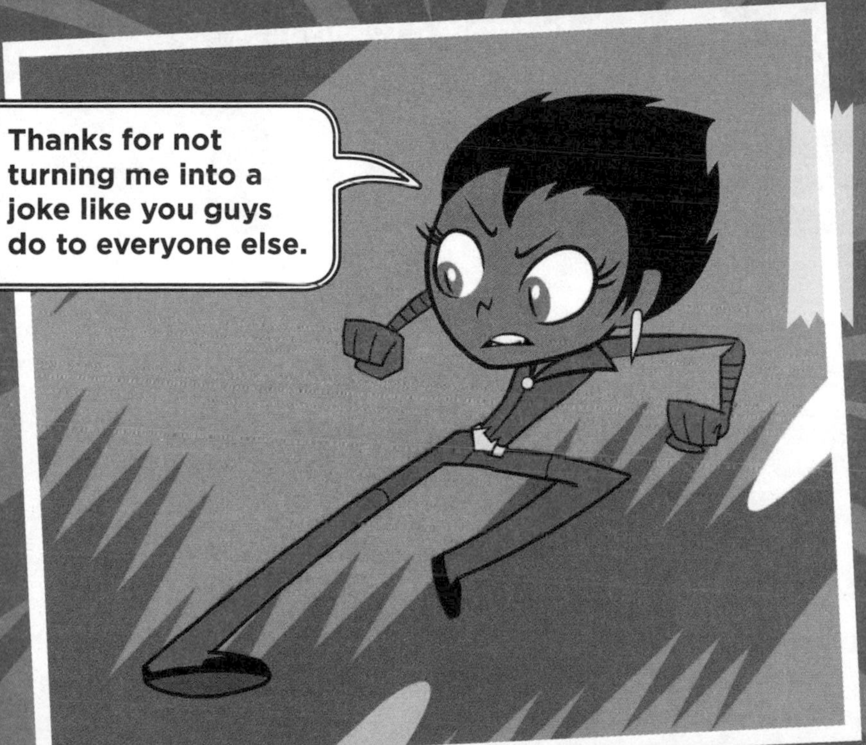

Thanks for not turning me into a joke like you guys do to everyone else.

You're...welcome....

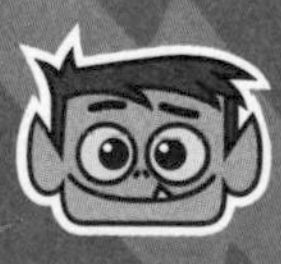

B'WANA BEAST

Hey. So. Um.

I hear you can take two different animals and combine them to create a totally new creature. That's cool.

B'wana hang out tonight?
(Beast Boy made me say that.)

I would, but I'm washing my hair.
(Beast Boy made me say that.)

DETECTIVE CHIMP

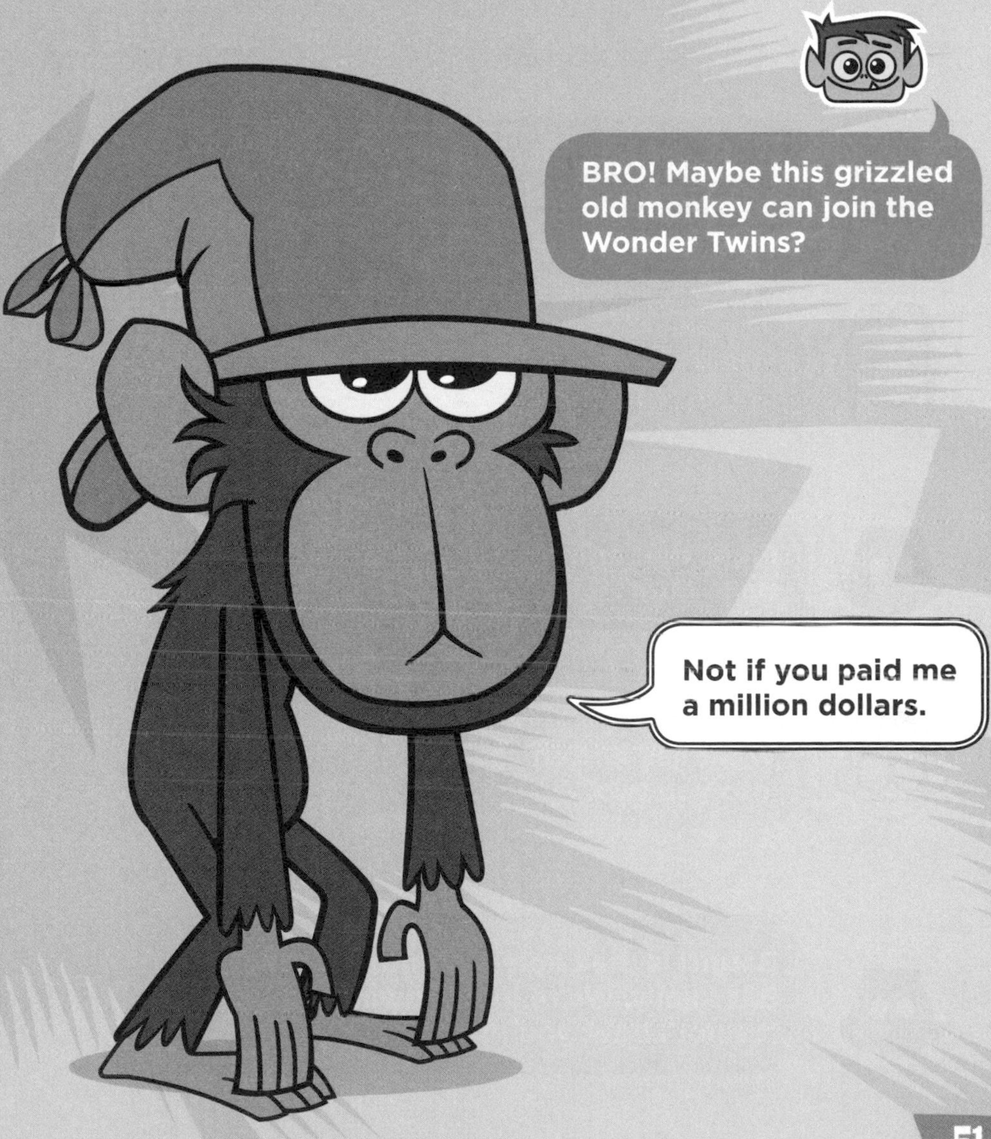
BRO! Maybe this grizzled old monkey can join the Wonder Twins?
Not if you paid me a million dollars.

BATGIRL

YASSSSSS, sister-friend, YASSSSSS!

Werk, werk, werk! Snap, snap, snap!

We are the LIVING for you!

Fight that crime, Babs gurl!

What has gotten into you two?

Batgirl is the coolest member of the Bat family. We're just showing support. It's not about you right now.

COMMISSIONER JAMES GORDON

Sweet 'stache, Commish!

Sniff, sniff. Whatchoo got stored in that thing?

A little bit of cold pizza and upper-lip sweat.

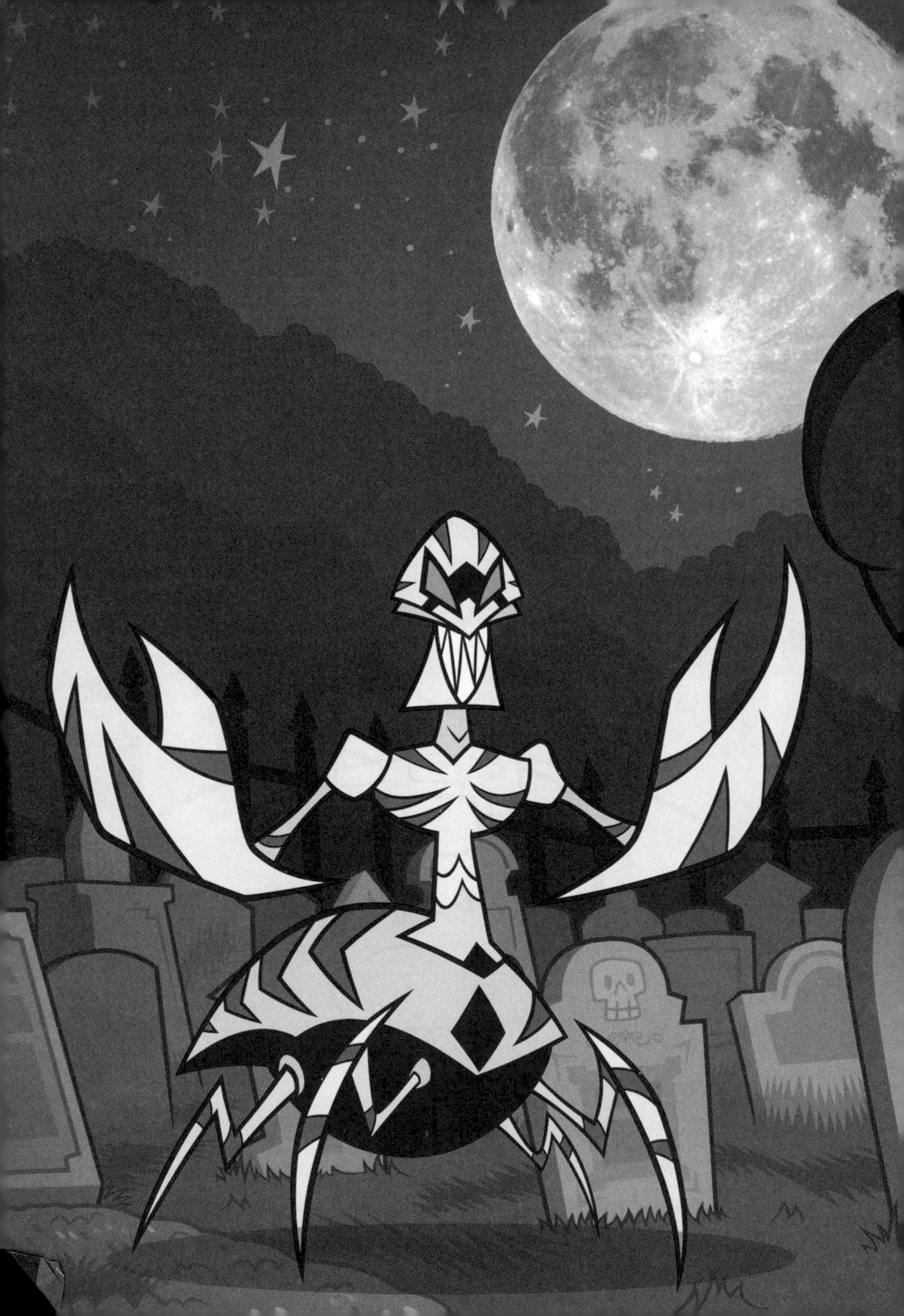

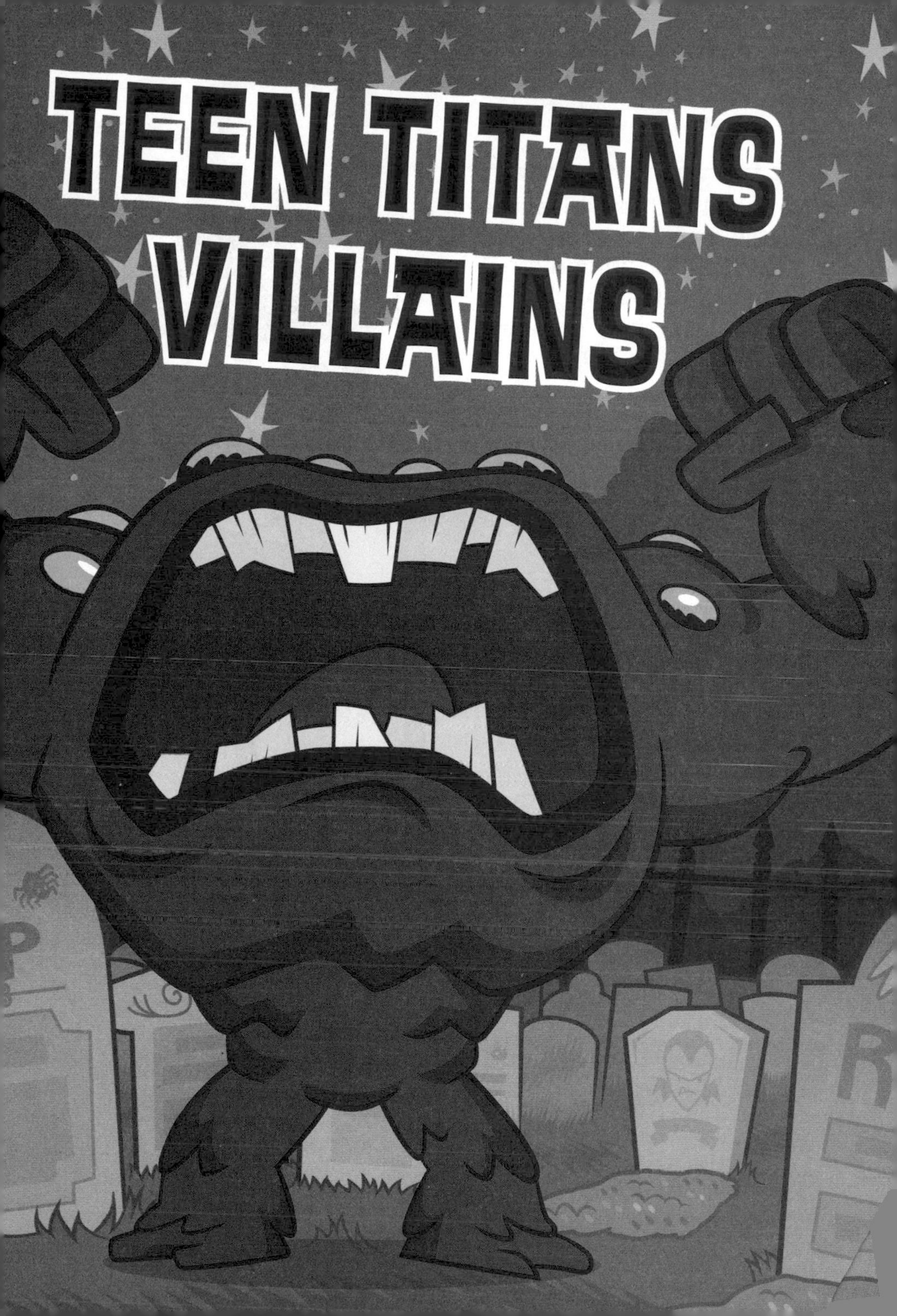
TEEN TITANS
VILLAINS

We deal with evil villains every single day. Some of them are harmless, misguided crooks. Others? Not so much. If I had a nickel for every galactic warlord we've fought...

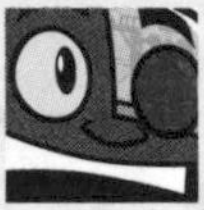

You'd have way less than a dollar.

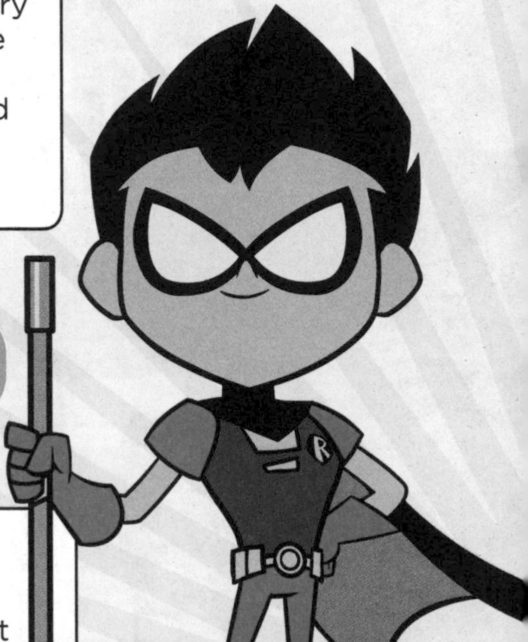

My point is, they all have the capacity to harm others. And for that reason, we must remain vigilant and stand against them! A hero must always study his enemy, even if that enemy is a gigantic, bumbling dummy.

Oh, we've definitely fought some *dummies.*

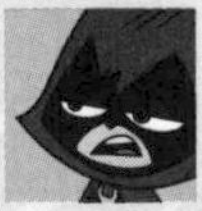

And some meanies.

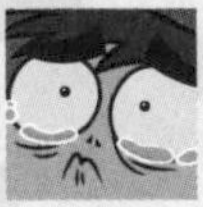

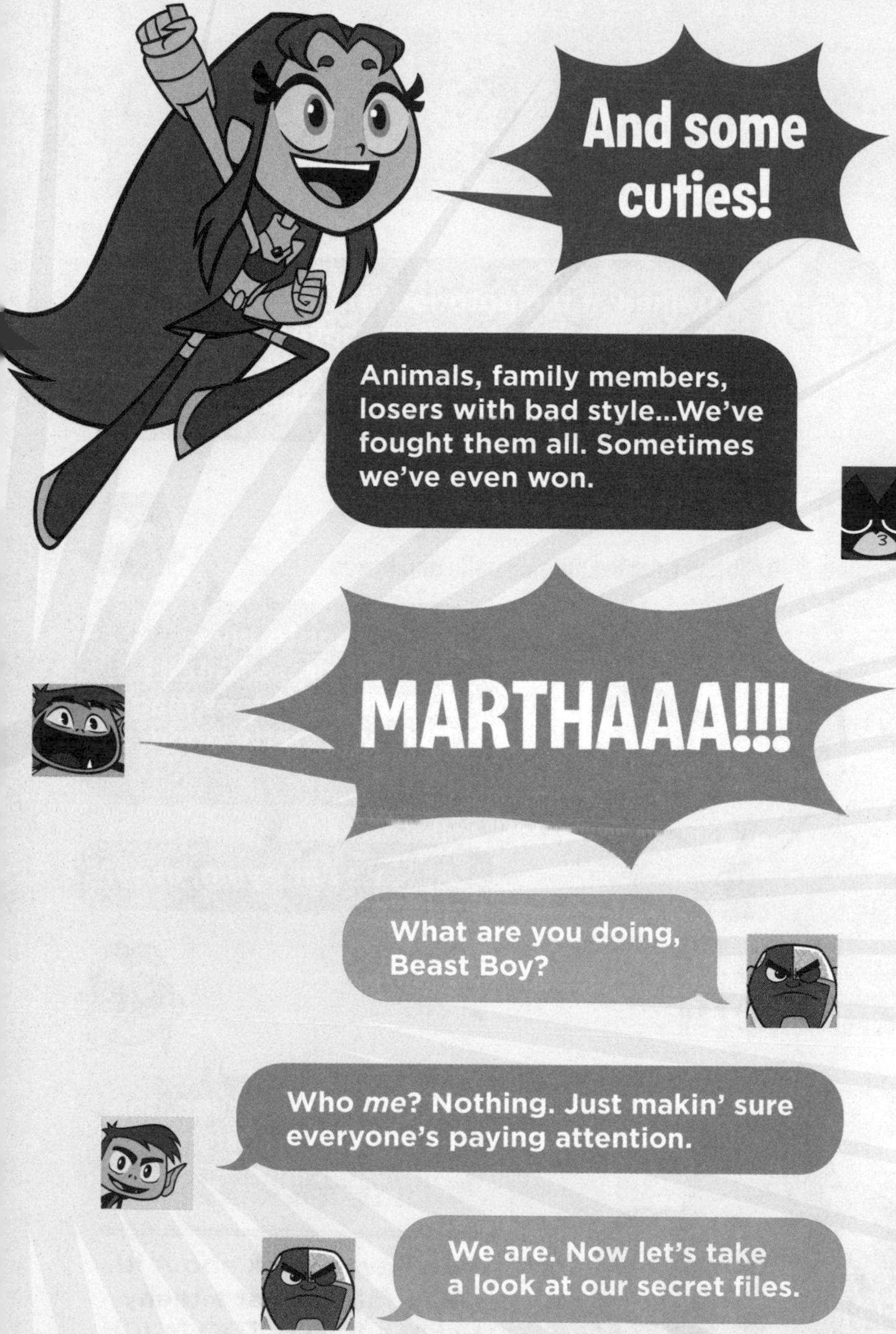
And some cuties!
Animals, family members, losers with bad style...We've fought them all. Sometimes we've even won.
MARTHAAA!!!
What are you doing, Beast Boy?
Who *me*? Nothing. Just makin' sure everyone's paying attention.
We are. Now let's take a look at our secret files.

H.I.V.E. FIVE

Trained at the notorious H.I.V.E. Academy, these five troublemakers have caused us a lot of headaches. And backaches. And tummyaches. Yeah, I'm sore about it.

JINX

Powers & Abilities: Creates magic spells and hexes

You've got to give Jinx her props. Get it? Because she does magic. That was pretty good, I think.

At least I'm *trying*, okay?

MAMMOTH

Powers & Abilities: Super-strength

The bigger they are, the more they are frightened of the tickling.

Don't even think about it! Okay, maybe just a teeny tickle but NOT TOO MUCH.

GIZMO

Powers & Abilities: Technological genius, inventor, team leader

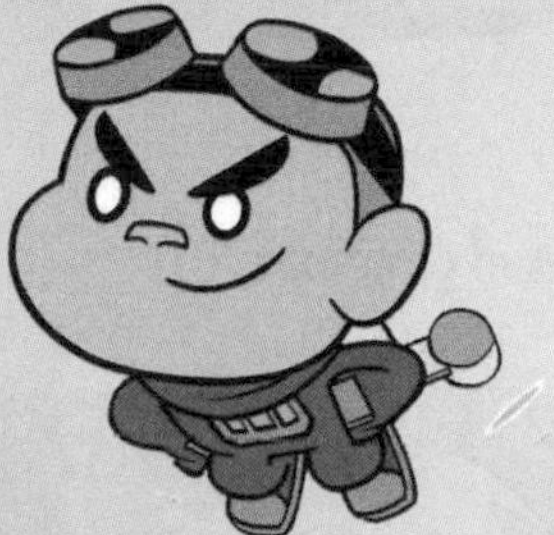

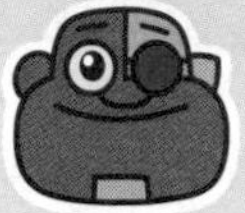

Awww, look at this angry little nugget!

I just wanna take one of his gadgets, use it to trap him in a never-ending techno-maze, and watch him struggle to get out.

BILLY NUMEROUS

Powers & Abilities: Can create clones of himself, can talk A LOT

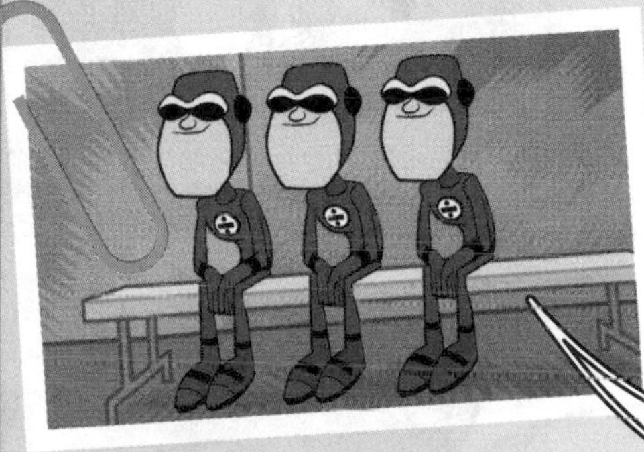

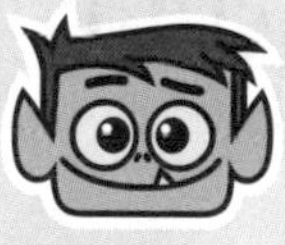

Bumpkin.

Beast.

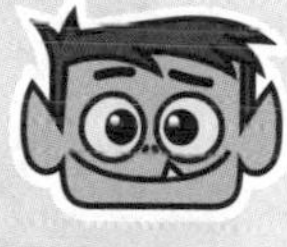

Rube.

...I got nothin'.

SEE-MORE

Powers & Abilities: Laser eye, flight, exceptional caricature artist

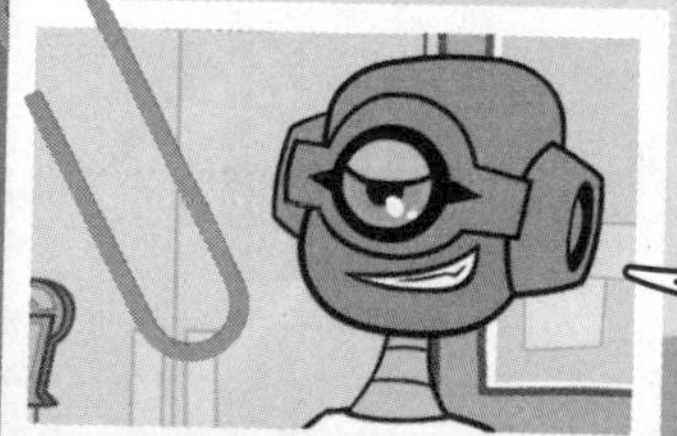

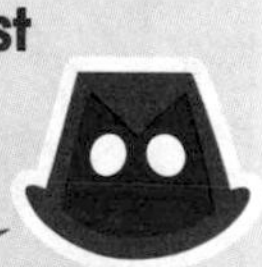

Draw me like one of your worst enemies.

Huh?

RAVAGER

Real Name: Rose Wilson

Powers & Abilities: Super-strength, trained gymnast, skilled martial artist

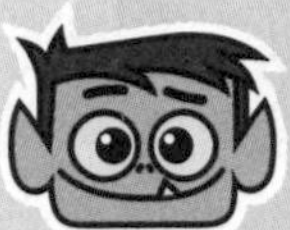

She *dangerous.*

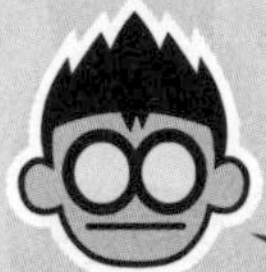

Of course she is.

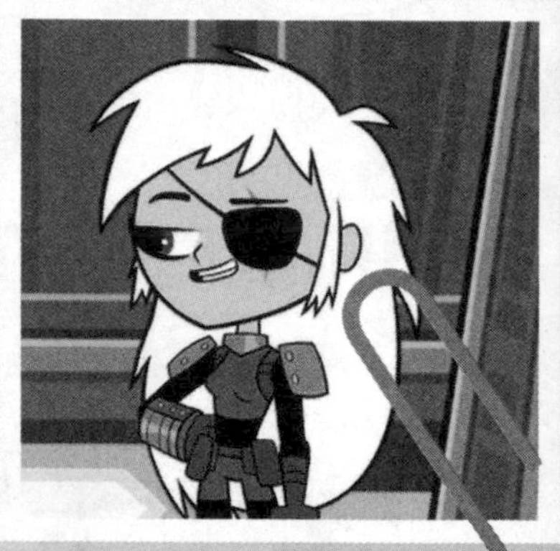

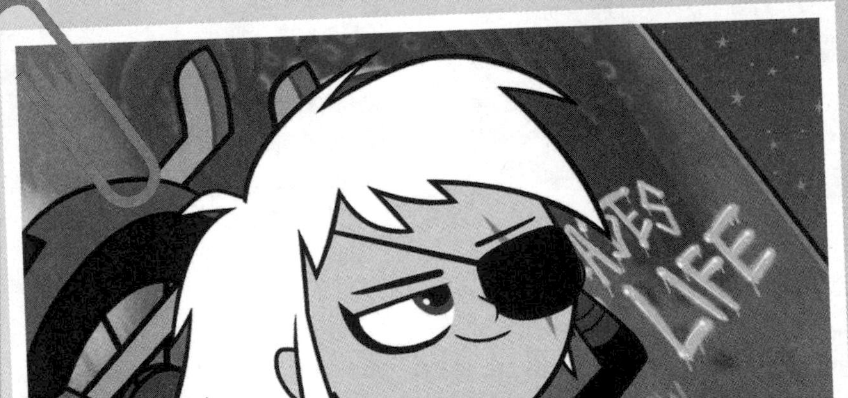
LIFE
MEOW

Never trust someone whose father is evil. *Never*. Never *ever*. Never *ever*, *ever*.

I beg to differ.

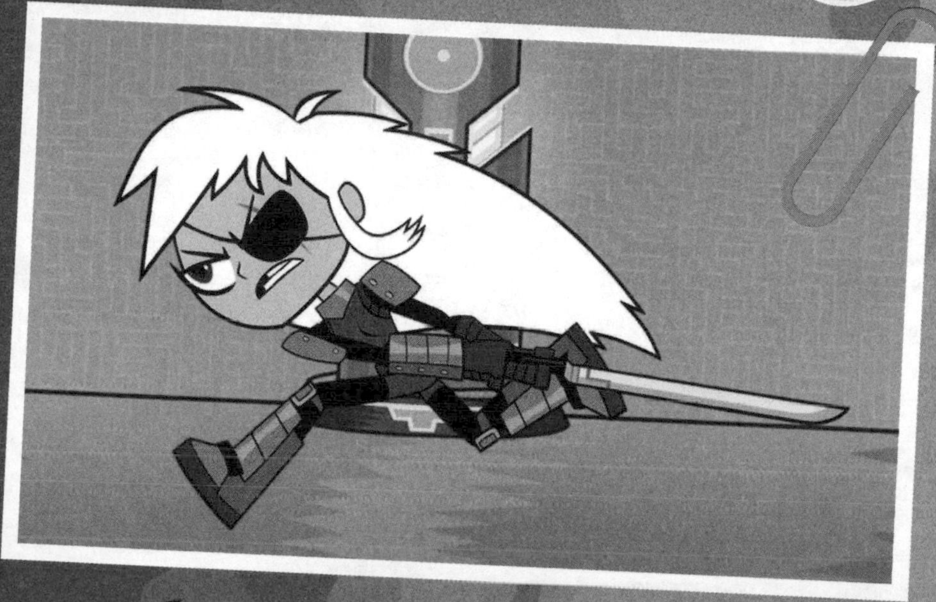

Katana blade *shiny*.

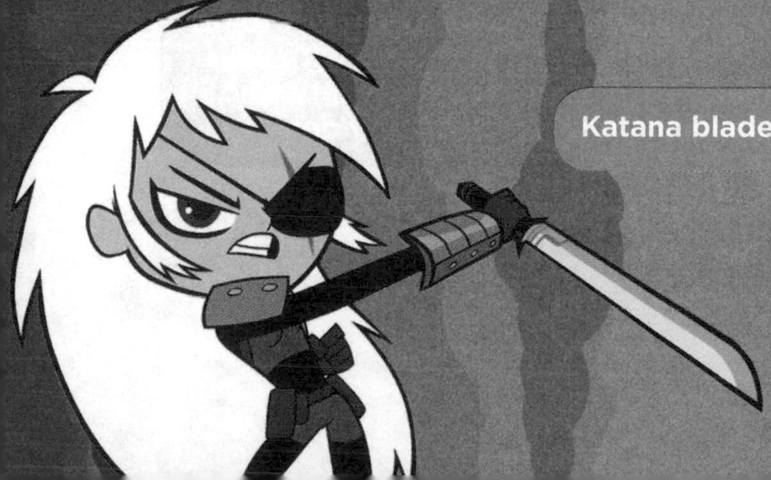

TERRA

Powers & Abilities: Control the earth through geokinesis, which allows her to move rocks with her mind

 Hey, girl, *hey*. Been a long time, my li'l *rock* star. Why so *stone*-faced?

 Cut it out, Beast Boy. Terra is not to be flirted with. She plays tricks with your mind. She's a menace to society who wants to *crush you with boulders*.

 You know me, Mama.

I'm supes crushable!

BLACKFIRE

Powers & Abilities: Fire off bursts of dark energy called blackbolts, super-strength, flight...basically all the same powers as Starfire

 My big sister and I do not always get along, but she is the family, and though we are different in many ways, I love her no matter what.

Ugh. Shut *up.*

 I do not shut up—I grow up, and when I look at your face, I SMILE BECAUSE YOU ARE BEAUTIFUL!

BROTHER BLOOD

Powers & Abilities: Mind control, super-intelligence, ability to be especially evil

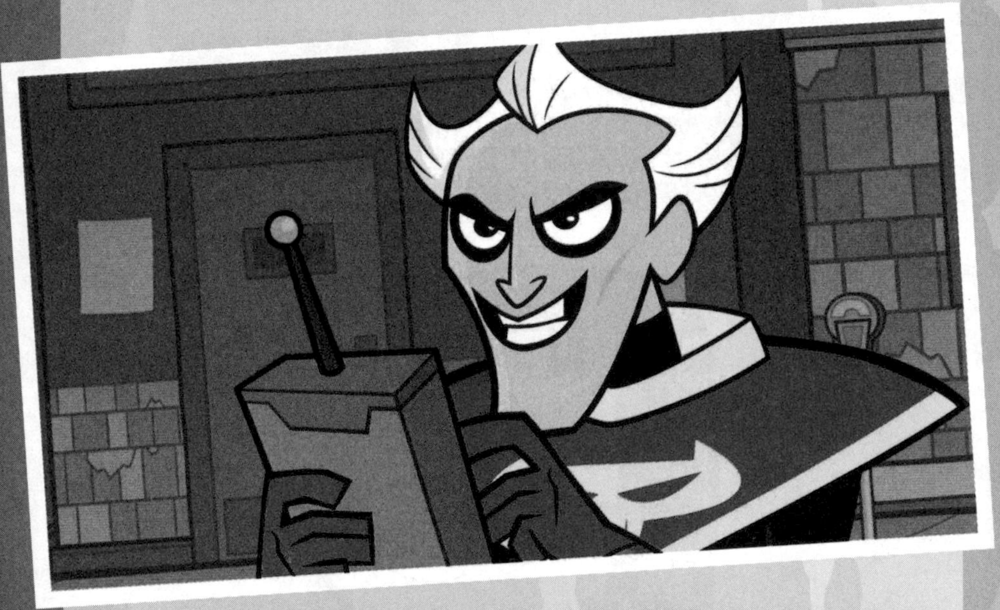

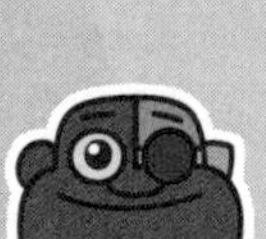

As headmaster of the H.I.V.E. Academy, Blood oversees a legion of budding little evildoers. He's also one of my archenemies. Dude thinks he's smarter than me.

Pshaw!

Just look at him. Weirdo. I'm not worried about it.

TRIGON

Powers & Abilities: Conquering; can devour souls, cast spells, and change shape; able to shoot fireballs

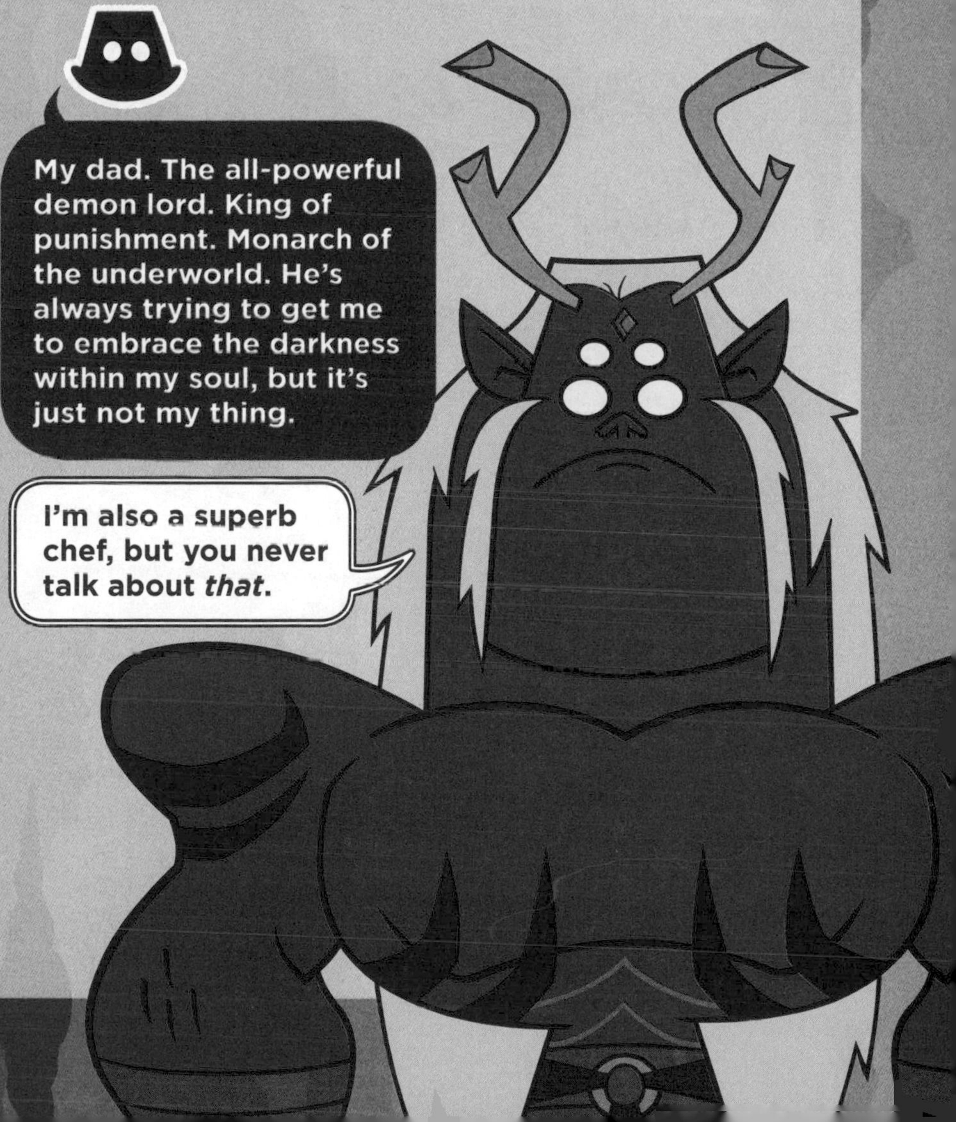
My dad. The all-powerful demon lord. King of punishment. Monarch of the underworld. He's always trying to get me to embrace the darkness within my soul, but it's just not my thing.
I'm also a superb chef, but you never talk about *that*.

THE BRAIN

Powers & Abilities: Super-intelligence, master strategist

 The Brain is so smart, it's scary. He always has some kind of nefarious plan up his sleeve.

Oooops!

I mean, up...his...brain? I don't know how to say this without offending armless and legless super-intellects.

 I wouldn't stress about it.

MONSIEUR MALLAH

Powers & Abilities: Super-strength

Mallah is the Brain's hopelessly devoted sidekick. He'll carry out whatever evil scheme his boss cooks up. These two do *not* like to be separated.

Nice beret, lah-hoo-zer.

You're the loser! This beret was made with fine, high-quality French felt!

KILLER MOTH

Powers & Abilities: Aptitude for super-science, hypnotism

 I do not like when the Killer Moth mutates poor, helpless, defenseless little pupae.

But! Without him, I would not have met my precious Silkie. *Ohhhh*, I can feel it. The emotions, they are happening. Now I am *the torn*.

 Heh-heh, *pupae*.

MOTHER MAE-EYE

Powers & Abilities: Hypnotism, mind control, ability to make *excellent* pies

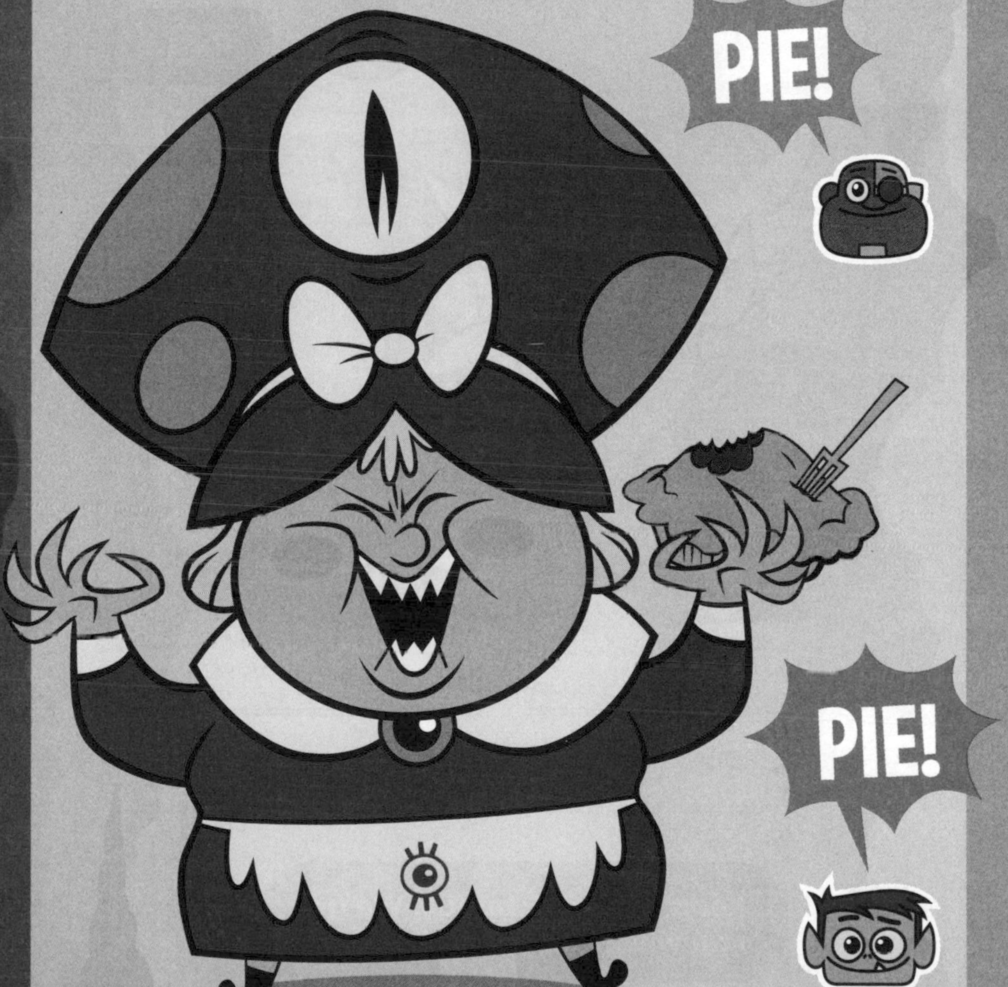
PIE!
PIE!

MUMBO JUMBO

Powers & Abilities: Magic, telekinesis, shape-shifting, teleportation

 Pass.

But...but...I'm a very dangerous magician!

 Keep it movin', buddy. We got real villains to get to here.

ROBOT OVERLORDS

Powers & Abilities: Energy blasts

Wait a minute. Why can't we call them *Manhunters*? That's their official name, right?

There's no need to gender a group of robots. Especially if they're robot *overlords* bent on destruction. After all, we don't call you *Mr.* Cyborg.

OooOooO! Call me *Mr.* Cyborg!

CINDERBLOCK

Powers & Abilities: Super-strength, durability

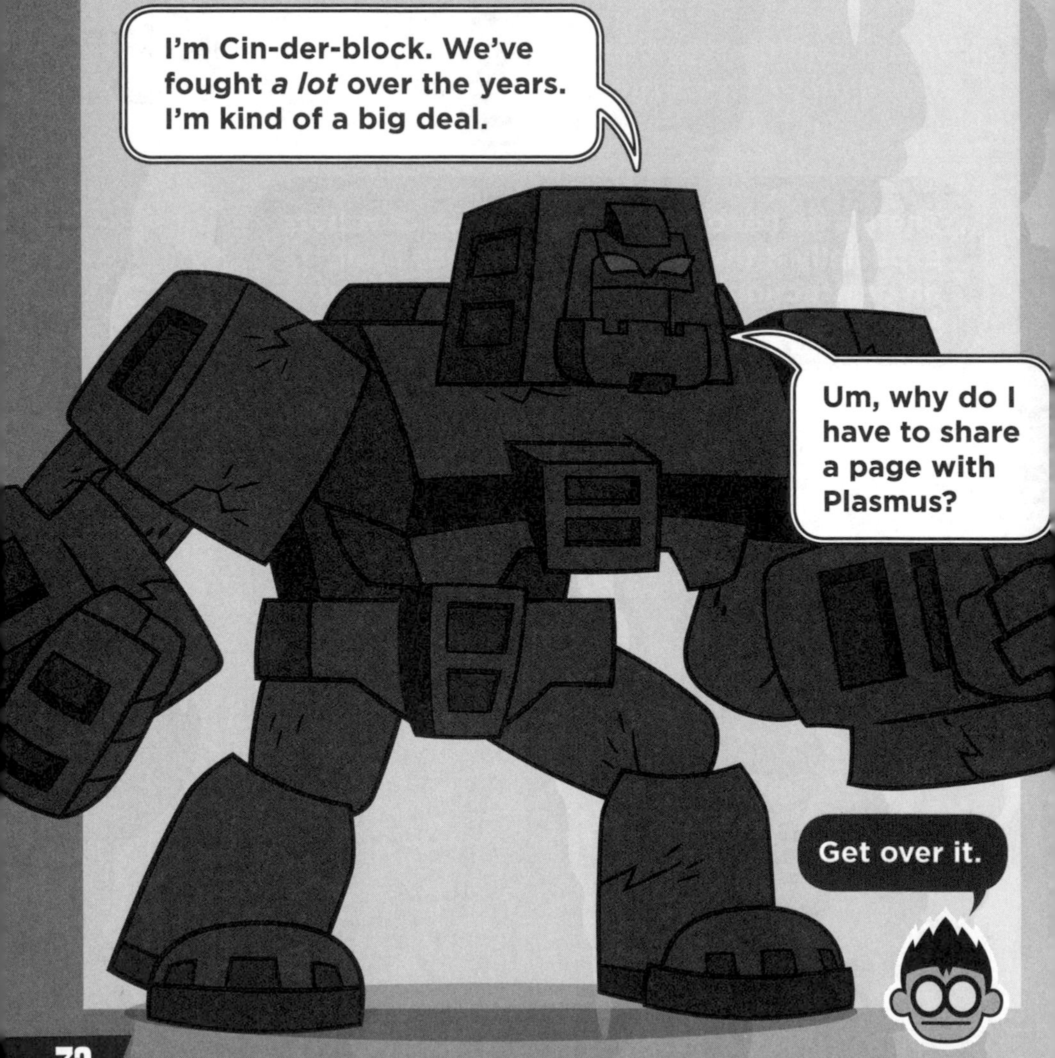
I'm Cin-der-block. We've fought *a lot* over the years. I'm kind of a big deal.
Um, why do I have to share a page with Plasmus?
Get over it.

PLASMUS

Powers & Abilities: Super-strength, invulnerability, limited shape-shifting, acidic saliva

Always be wary of an ugly sludge monster with a bad attitude whose slobber can burn you to a crisp.

Ugly?

You heard me.

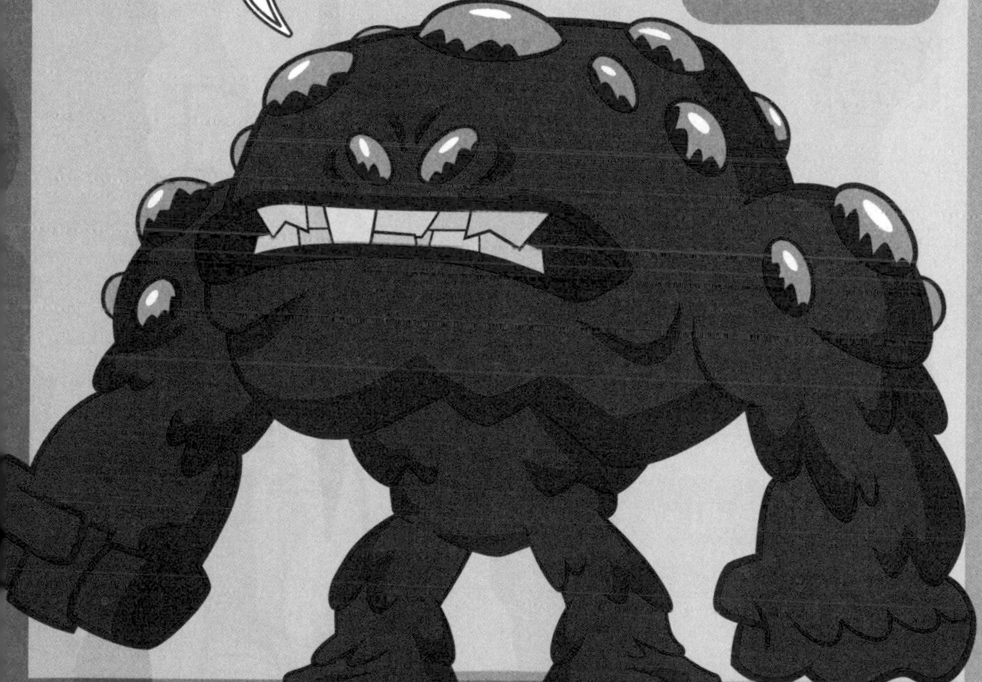

DR. LIGHT

Powers & Abilities: Wears a high-tech suit that allows him to harness the power of light

He's trash.

Oh my, yes. He is the garbage person.

Did somebody say *garbage*? Cuz my tummy is rumblin'.

I can hear you.

We know.

And we do not the care!

KILLER CROC

Powers & Abilities: Super-strength, sharp teeth and claws

Killer Croc?! Yer killin' me, bro. Where's *Harley Quinn*?

Harley Quinn isn't one of our signature villains.

Yeah, but she's popular! And spicy.

I suppose. If you're into that kind of razzle-dazzle. No offense, Croc.

No, she's way more popular than me. I totally get it.

KITTEN

Powers & Abilities: Middling bank robber, humongous brat

KITTIES! KITTIES!

No, Starfire. This is *Kitten*, Killer Moth's daughter. She's *bad*.

THE BAD KITTY! *NOOOOOO!*

Trigon, Slade, Killer Moth. We fight a lot of evil dads and daughters.

AHEM! Oh wait. That *is* weird.

CONTROL FREAK

Powers & Abilities: Technological genius, encyclopedic knowledge of television

This guy is the worst. Control Freak is great with electronics, but all he does is use his skills to try to destroy the Titans. What a waste of talent.

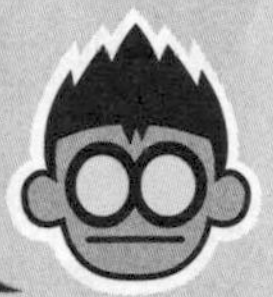

You wouldn't be here if it weren't for me! I was the one who first broke THE FOURTH WALL. You all owe your entire existence to me!

Can you believe this guy, gentle readers?

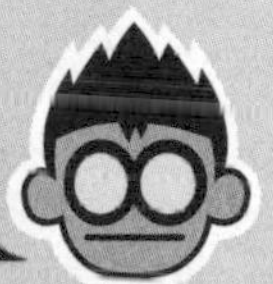

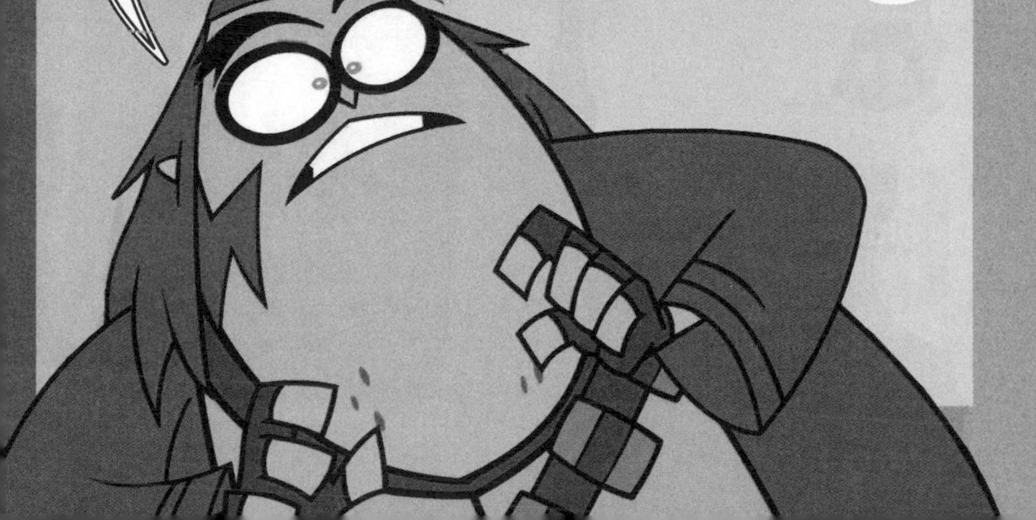

KYD WYKKYD

Powers & Abilities: Teleportation, skilled hand-to-hand combat

What a poser. Thinks he's some kind of avenger of the night.

He doesn't have a cave or a car. Where's his Utility Belt? Nowhere.

He's just a fan with time on his hands. Makes me sick.

Never trust anyone with more than two *y*'s in their name.

DEATH

Powers & Abilities: Soul collector

Oh. Look. It's my jolly godfather. *Death.*

What's up, Rae-Rae! Want to go steal people's spirits?

I'm busy. And don't call me Rae-Rae.

Fair enough.

SQUIRREL

Powers & Abilities: Expert nut-tracker

I AM HAVING THE CUTE OVERLOAD!

Somebody get the fainting couches.

MAD MOD

Powers & Abilities: Inventor, hypnotist, time traveler, can use his cane to steal people's youth

Check out them nasty chompers, guv.

Dental hygiene is very important to most people but clearly not Mad Mod.

C'mere and give us a kiss, luvvies.

GAAAHHHHH!
MONSTER SMOOCHES!
GET IT AWAY
FROM ME!

PUNK ROCKET

Powers & Abilities: Can create devastating hypersonic waves using his guitar

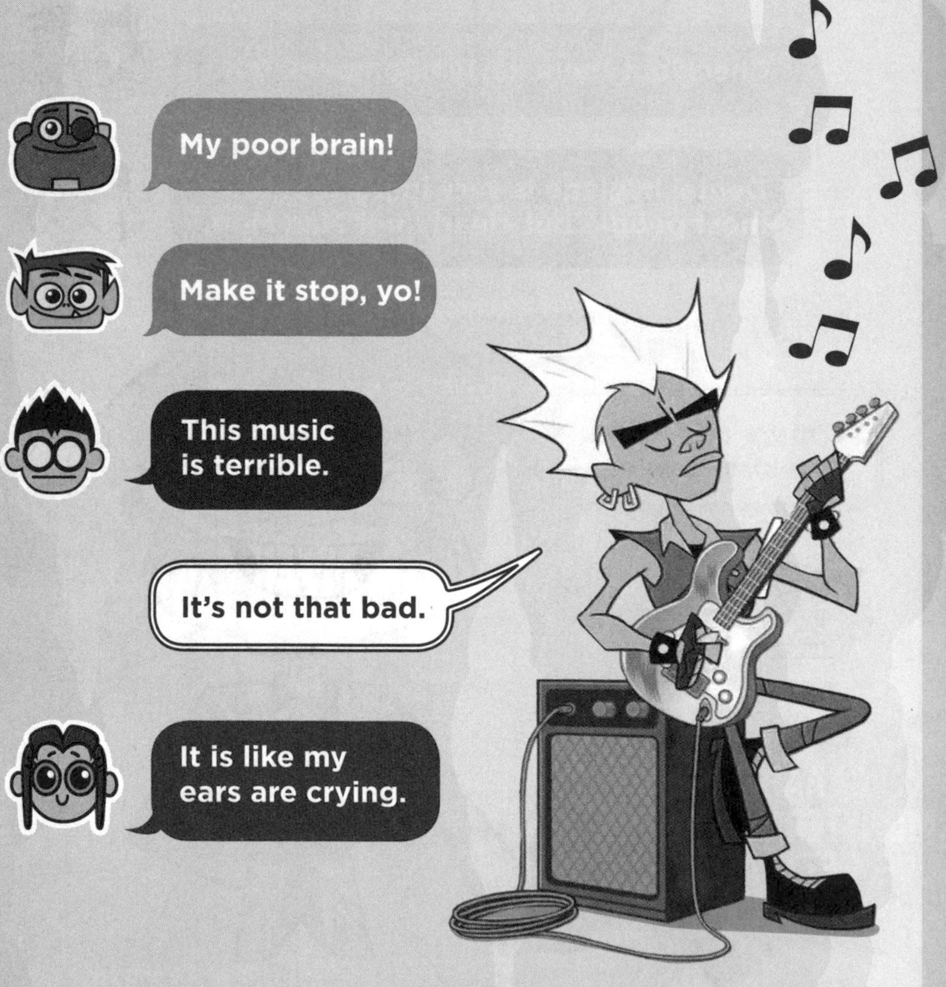
My poor brain!
Make it stop, yo!
This music is terrible.
It's not that bad.
It is like my ears are crying.

THE MAGIC GOD

Powers & Abilities: Magic, duh

What a joke. He's neither magical nor a god, and he doesn't respect *actual sorcery.* More like Magic FRAUD. That was a good one, right? Raven's got zingers, guys.

Wait. Now I'm doing the third person. SIGH. When is this thing over?

Eeep!

I want to shower this cutie with the cuddles.

DARKSEID

Powers & Abilities: Cosmic tyranny, super-strength, can fire Omega beams from his eyes

 Ah yes. Dark warlord of the planet Apokolips. From his home world, Darkseid commands a fleet of frightening shock troops known as Parademons.

 He is not the nice!

 What she said.

 Those Omega beams of his will find you wherever you're hiding—the closet, under the bed, behind a pile of pizza crusts that everyone wants you to clean up but you won't because it's a cool fort you built to show people how resourceful you are with food waste.

 Gimme dat FOOD WASTE!

Can I just say something, please? You people don't know me, *okay.* All this name-calling and "oh, he's a dark warlord who'll shoot me with his laser eyes" isn't fair.

You don't know what I've been through. It's actually very difficult being me, and I wish you guys gave me a little credit every once in a while.

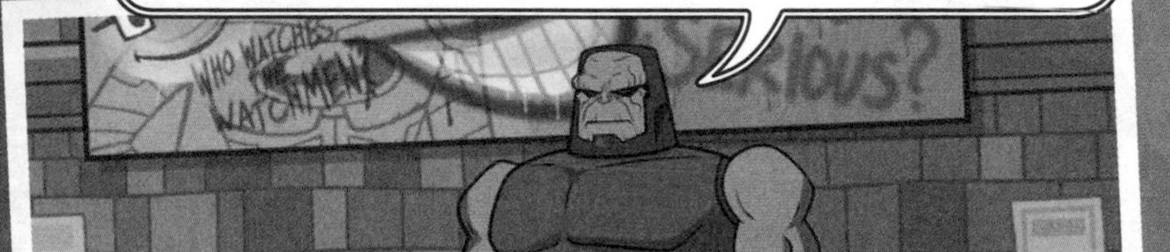
WHO WATCHES THE WATCHMEN
NO LITTERING

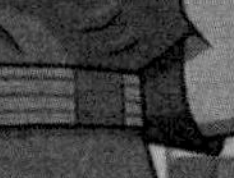

Really, dude?

No. I'll destroy you all without a second thought. Darkseid gotta Darkseid.

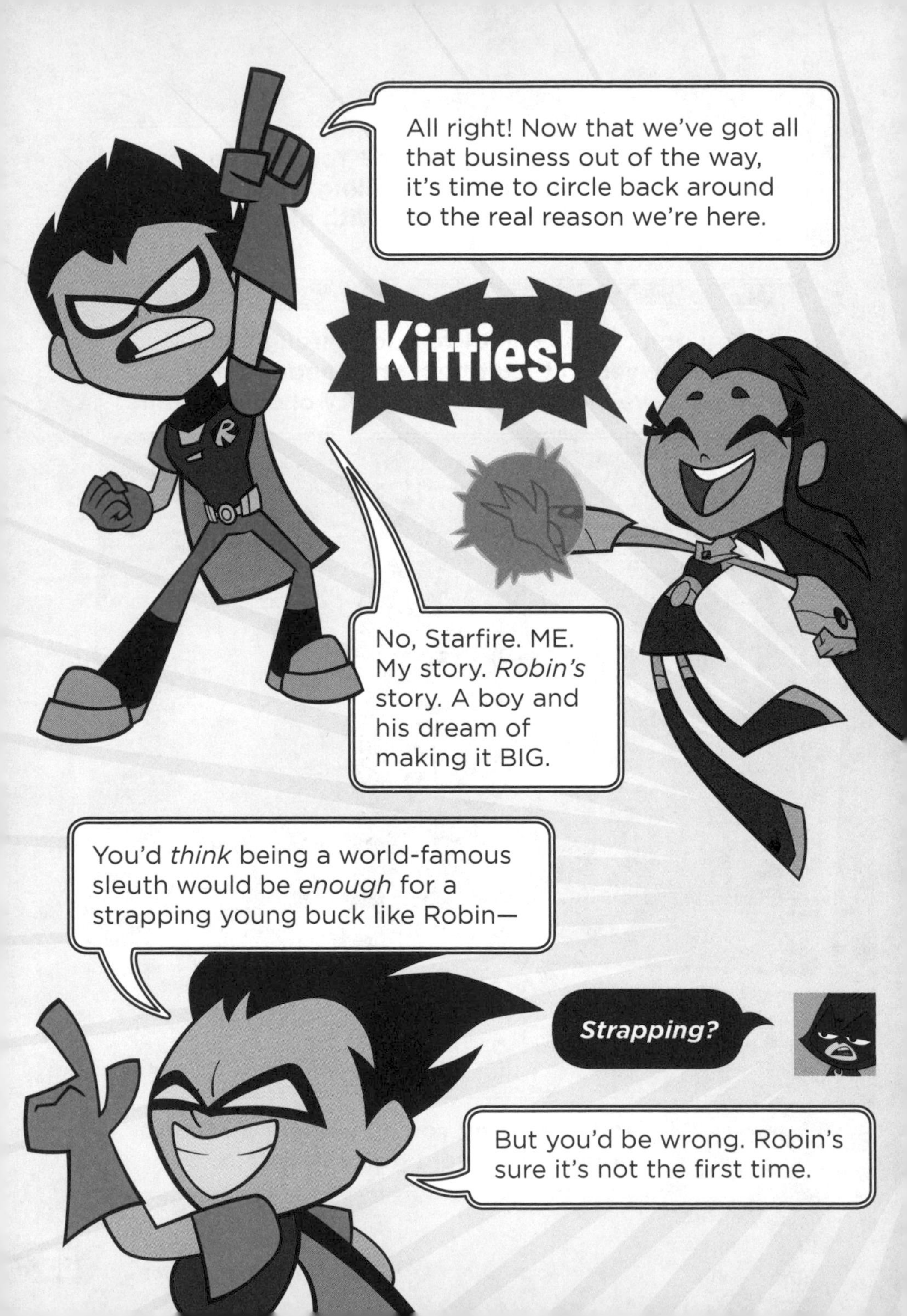

All right! Now that we've got all that business out of the way, it's time to circle back around to the real reason we're here.
Kitties!
No, Starfire. ME. My story. *Robin's* story. A boy and his dream of making it BIG.
You'd *think* being a world-famous sleuth would be *enough* for a strapping young buck like Robin—
Strapping?
But you'd be wrong. Robin's sure it's not the first time.

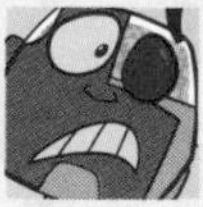

Uh, did we establish who he's talking to here? Or should I call one of his therapists?

See, Robin wasn't prepared to confront reality. Robin had an itch. Some might call it a hankerin'—

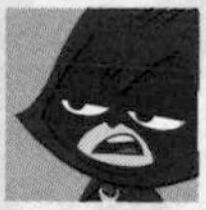

I don't think anyone would call it that. Also, why are you talking in third person?

BE. QUIET. Please. I'm sharing here.

I needed to become something more than a sidekick. I had to get out from under the shadow of the Bat. The only way to do *that* was to star in my very own super hero movie! Thankfully I found inspiration in a very special group of people. Timeless icons whose courage and determination serve as inspiration for younger generations. Allow me to introduce you to the World's Greatest Super Heroes...

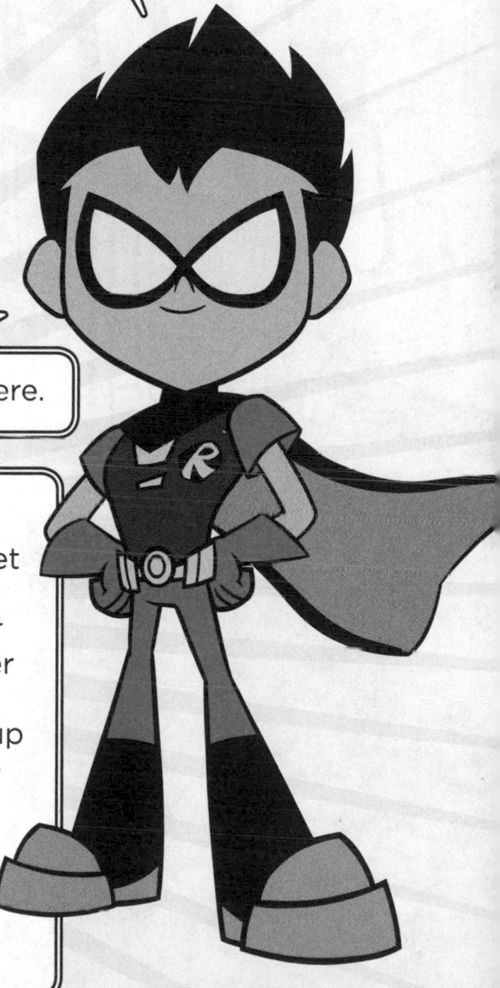

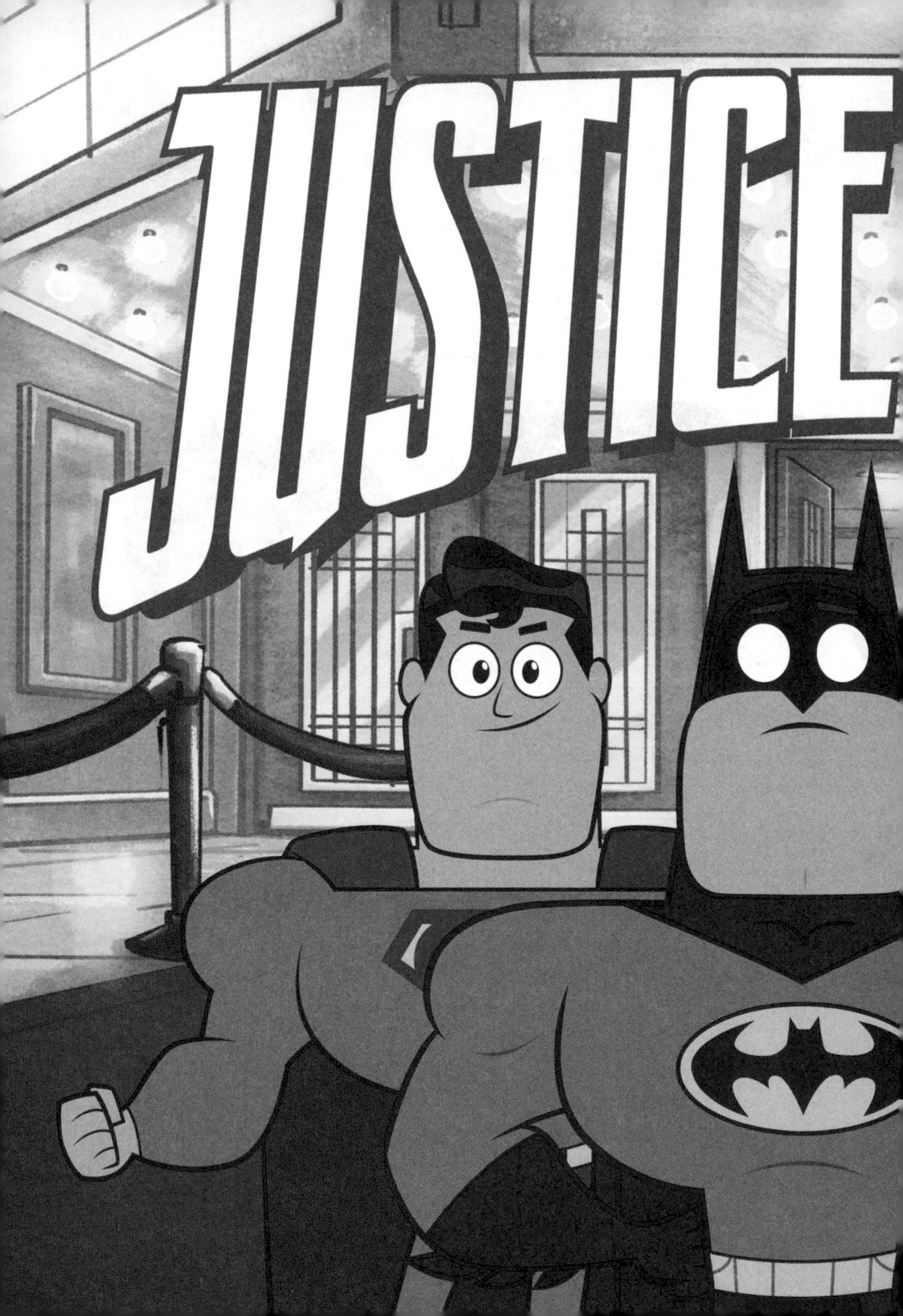
JUSTICE

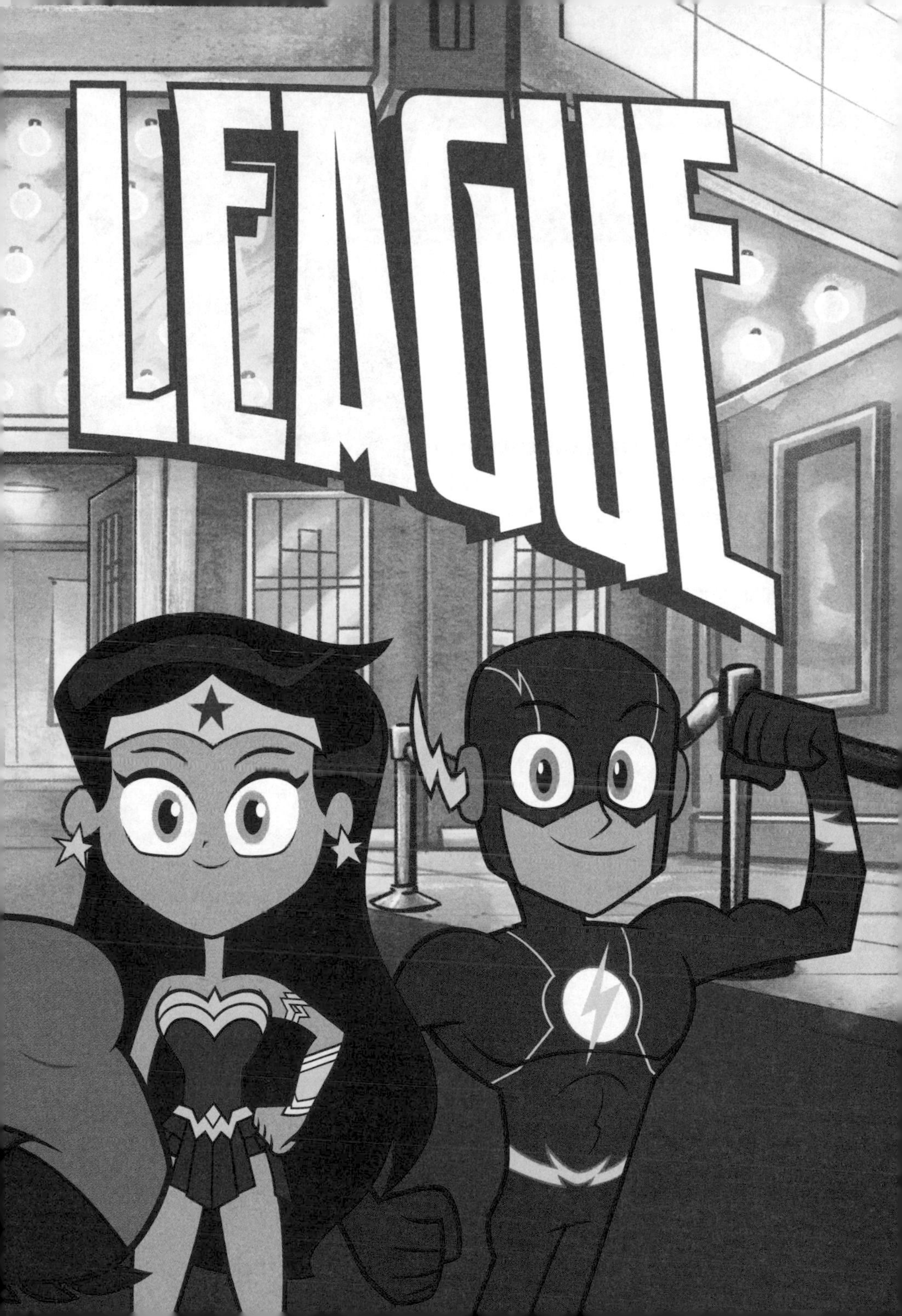
LEAGUE

SUPERMAN

Real Name: Kal-El

Nicknames: Man of Steel, Last Son of Krypton

Powers & Abilities: Invulnerability, super-strength, flight, super-speed, freeze breath, heat vision, X-ray vision

Archnemesis: Lex Luthor

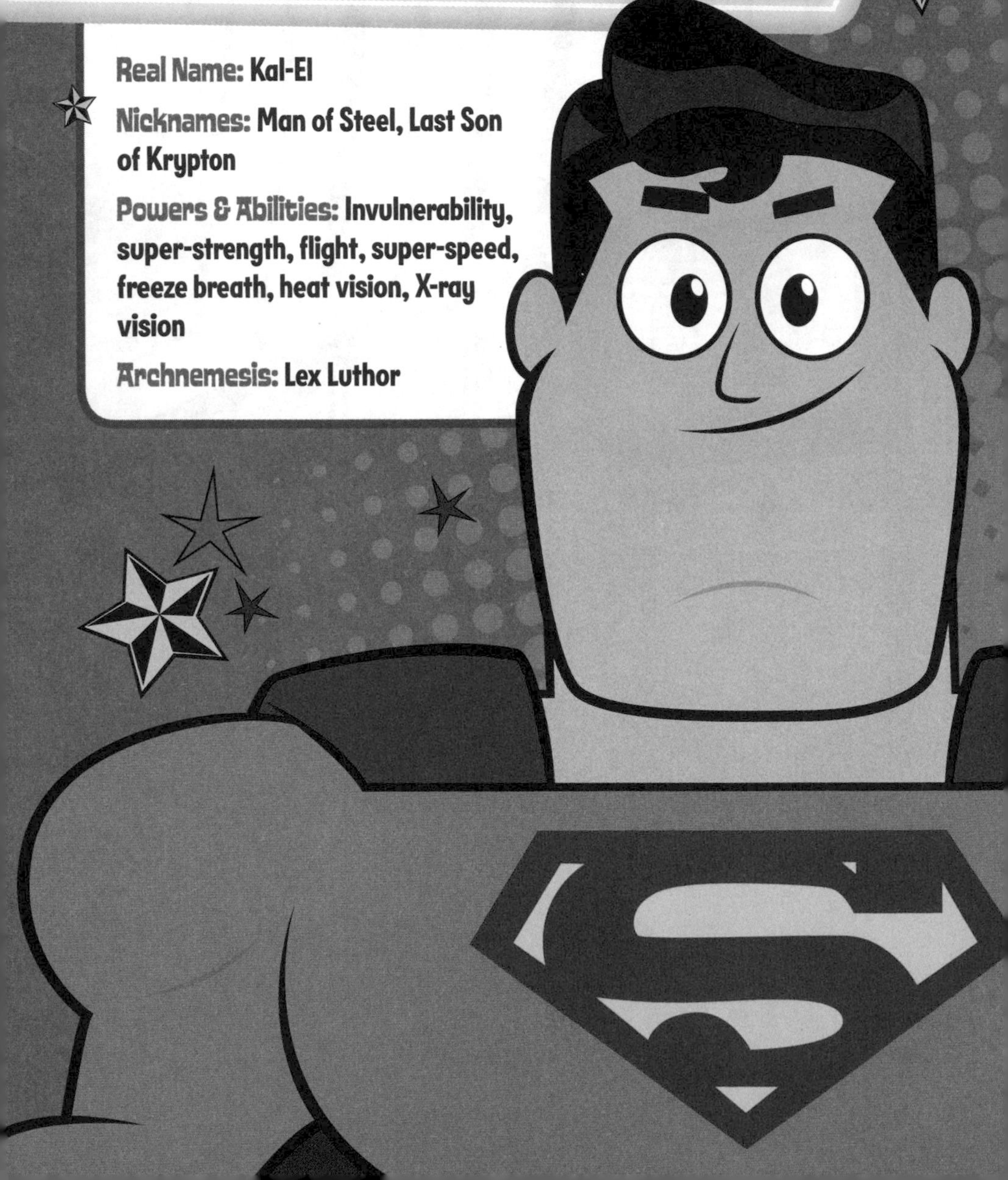

First up, we've got...

Superman don't need no flimsy introductions, dude. He's the King Daddy of the Super People! Everyone knows that. RESPECT HIS POW-AHHH.

As a boy growing up on my family's farm in Kansas, I knew I wasn't like other little kids. I had powers beyond my wildest imagination—super-strength, heat vision, and I could fly! Totally random, right?

Don't worry, I only used my abilities for good. Cat stuck in a tree? I'm your guy. Lid stuck on a jar of mayo? Call me. Then I found out I'm an alien from the planet Krypton, and things got even crazier. Eventually I moved to Metropolis, started working as a reporter for the *Daily Planet*, and embarked on a life of super heroism. Never looked back!

 Whoop, whoop! Superman!

 I can'ts believe it's him!

 Right?

WONDER WOMAN

Real Name: Diana Prince

Nicknames: Amazing Amazon, Warrior Princess

Powers & Abilities: Invulnerability, super-strength, flight, super-speed, trained fighter

Archnemesis: Cheetah

Raven, why don't *you* tell us Wonder Woman's origin story?

Sure thing. It all began when—

THE WONDER WOMAN AND I ARE PRACTICALLY SISTERS. She, too, is a princess! *I* did not grow up on an island full of Amazonian warriors, but oh, what a dream that would have been.

Can you imagine being surrounded by so many strong females? How inspiring! So much of the butt-kicking! But the butt-kicking was not enough to hold the princess's attention. She craved adventure beyond her island home. *OooOoooO*, the adventure! She went out into the world as Wonder Woman, champion of peace!

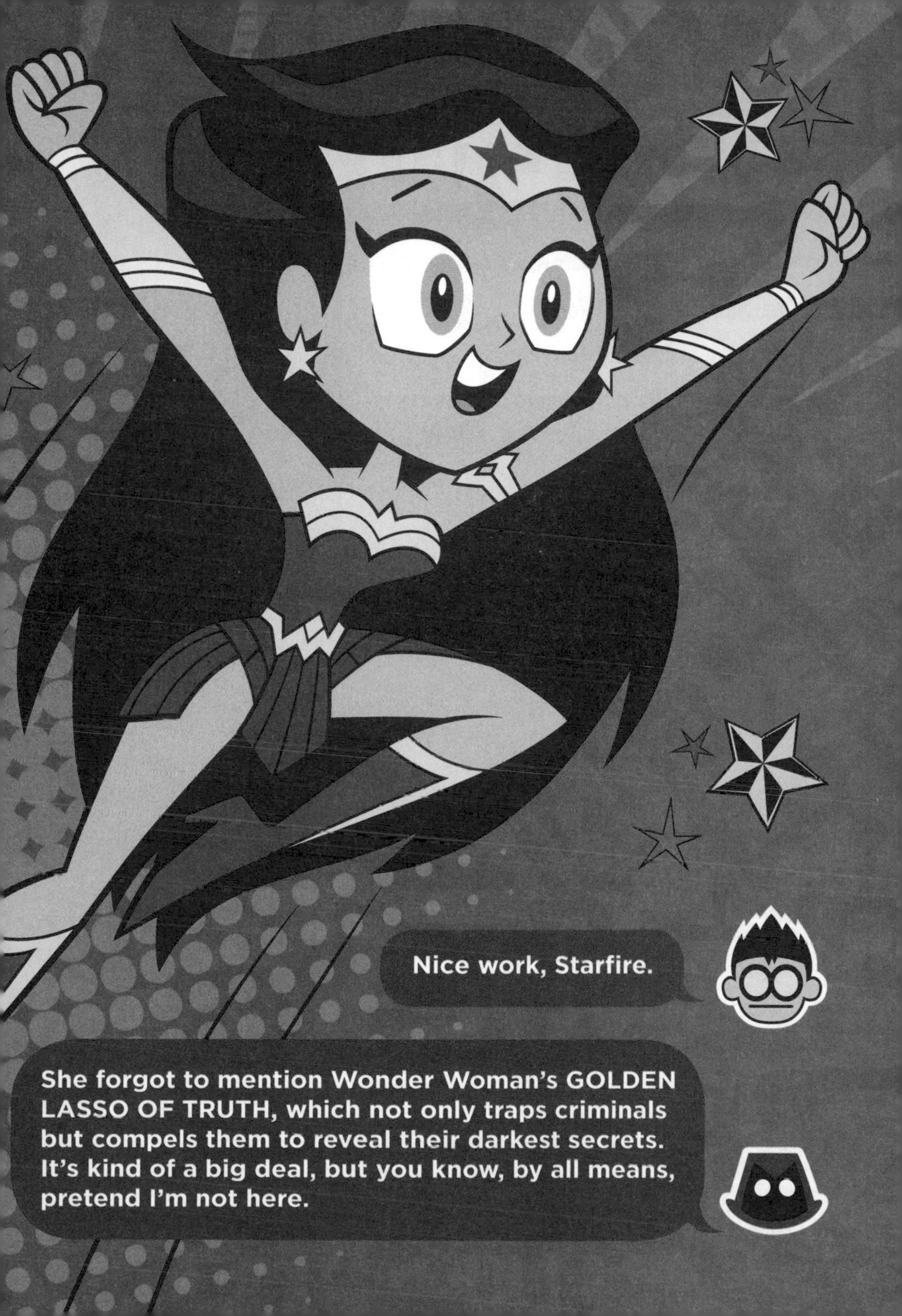
Nice work, Starfire.
She forgot to mention Wonder Woman's GOLDEN LASSO OF TRUTH, which not only traps criminals but compels them to reveal their darkest secrets. It's kind of a big deal, but you know, by all means, pretend I'm not here.

GREEN LANTERN

Real Name: John Stewart

Nicknames: Emerald Warrior

Powers & Abilities: Creation of constructs with Green Lantern power ring, skilled fighter, tactician

Archnemesis: Sinestro

My man! THIS IS THE STUFF.

He's so green!

Look at him. MY HERO. A knight in shining green armor wearing the universe's most powerful weapon all snug on his finger. DOES IT GET ANY BETTER?!

Speaking of space weapons, you ever find my Eternity Sleeve?

Not ringing any bells.

SWEET. My copyright lawyer can finally chill!

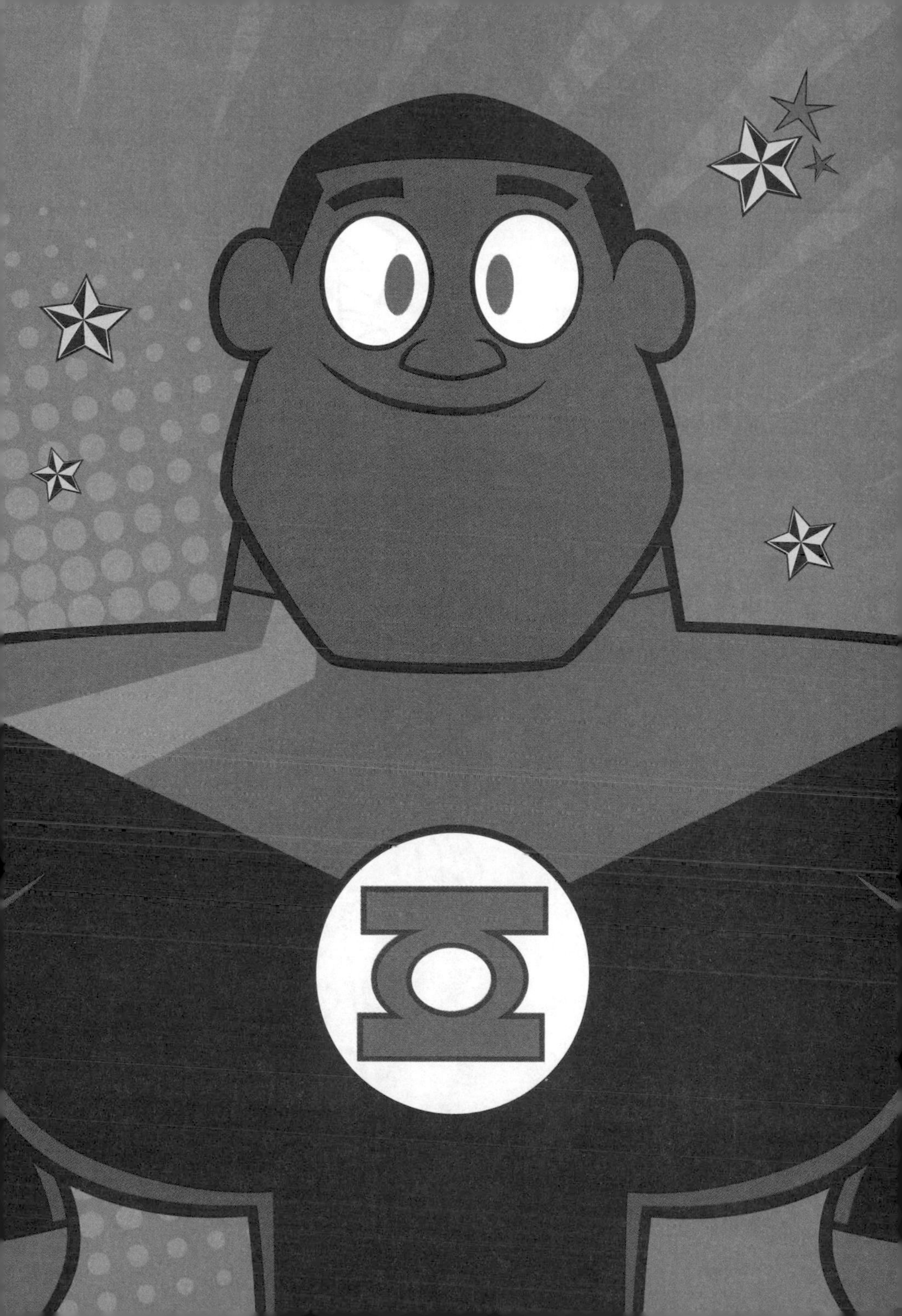

AQUAMAN

Real Name: Arthur Curry

Powers & Abilities: Telepathy, invulnerability, super-strength skilled fighter

Aquaman deserves our respect and admiration. As the king of Atlantis, he oversees Earth's oceans, which cover 70 percent of the planet. That's no easy task.

He also smells like fish.

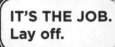

IT'S THE JOB. Lay off.

THE FLASH

Real Name: Barry Allen

Powers & Abilites: Super-speed, forensics, super-duper-speed

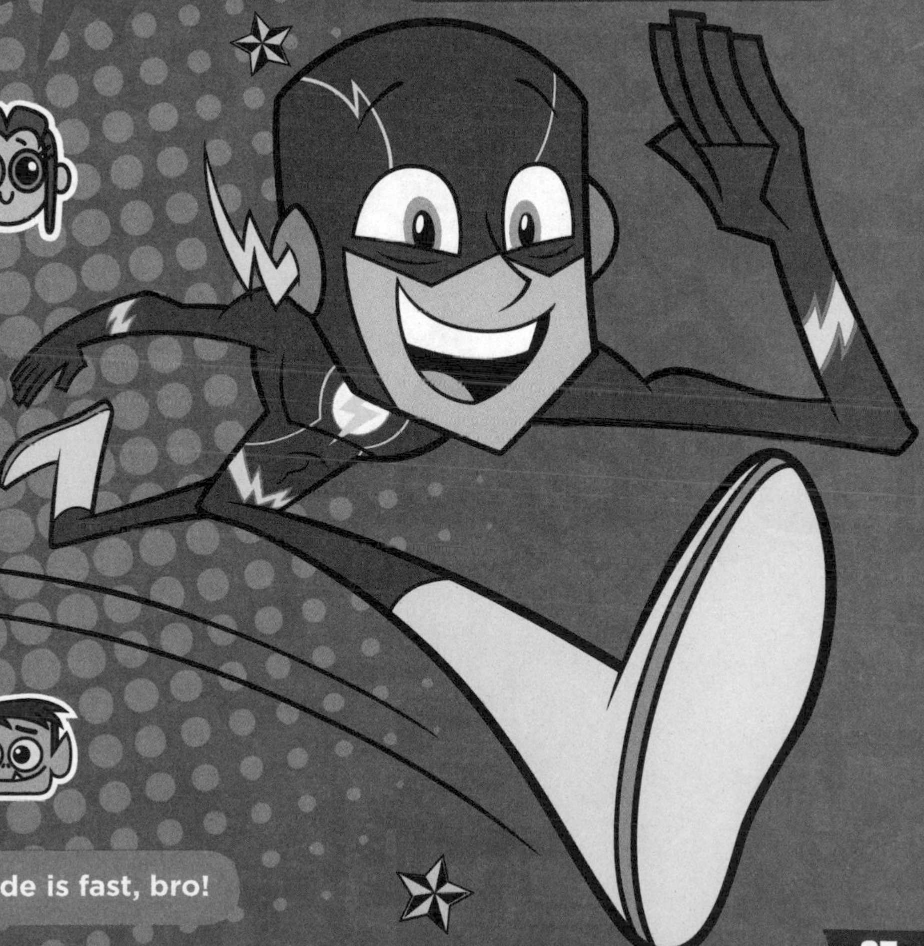

Flash! Flash!
Flash! Flash!
Flash! Flash!

Dude is fast, bro!

PLASTIC MAN

Real Name: Eel O'Brian
Powers & Abilities: Can stretch his body into various shapes and forms

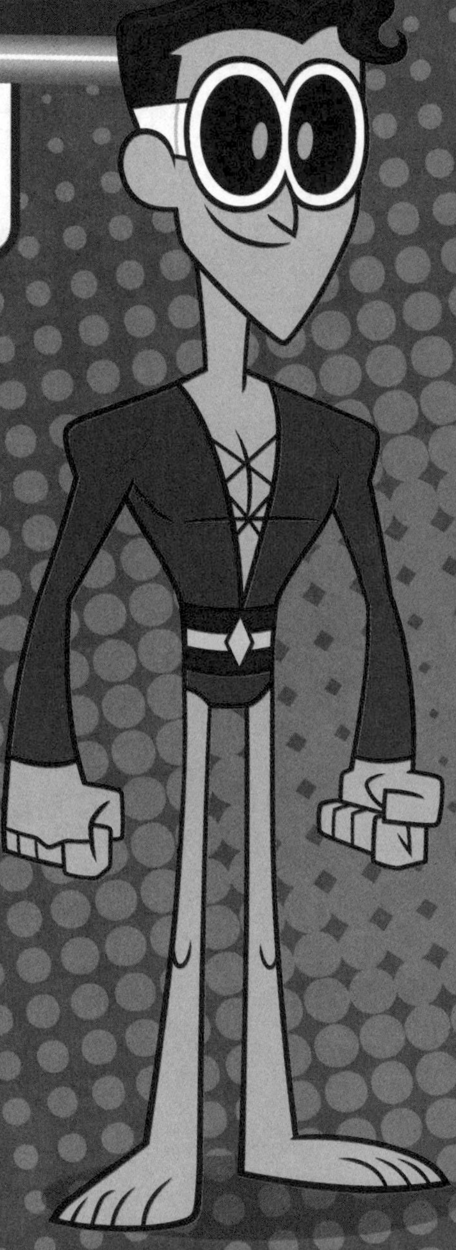

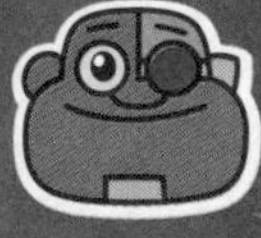

This is freaky.

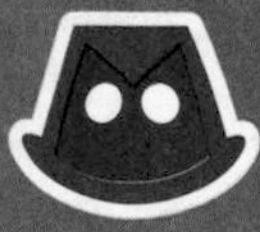

Yeeeaaahhh. It's making me very uncomfortable.

SUPERGIRL

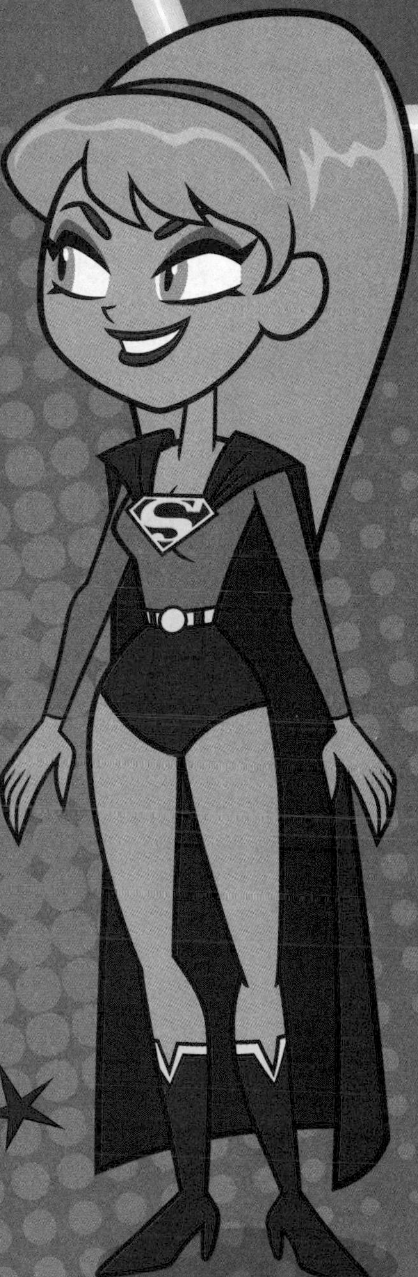

Real Name: Kara Zor-El

Powers & Abilities: Invulnerability, super-strength, flight, super-speed, freeze breath, heat vision, X-ray vision

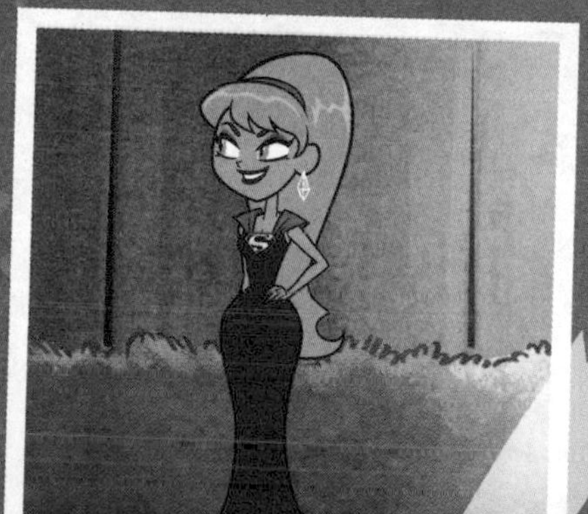

Whoop, whoop! Girls' night out!

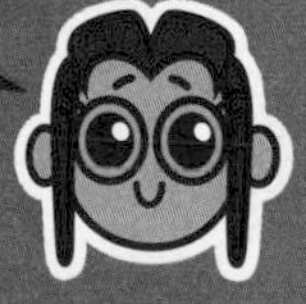

MARTIAN MANHUNTER

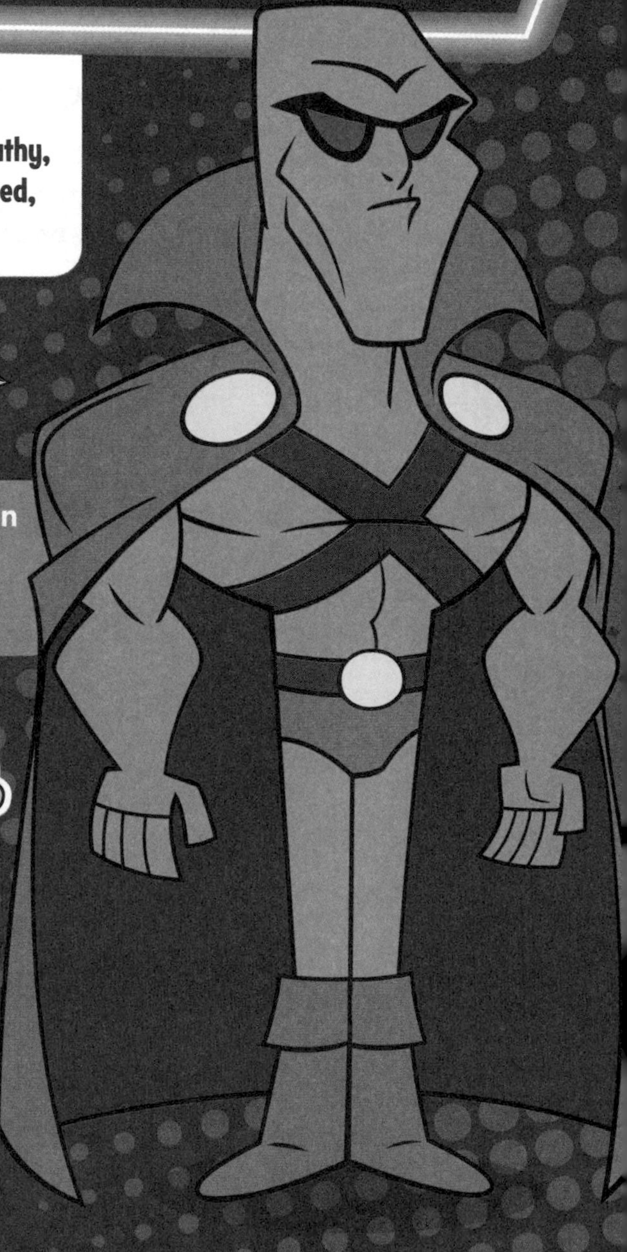

Real Name: J'onn J'onzz

Powers & Abilities: Telepathy, super-strength, super-speed, invisibility, Martian vision

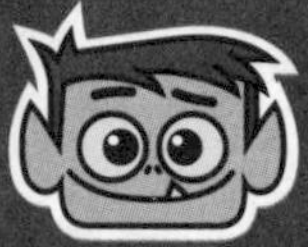

That's not the Martian Manhunter, fool! That's me *as* the Martian Manhunter.

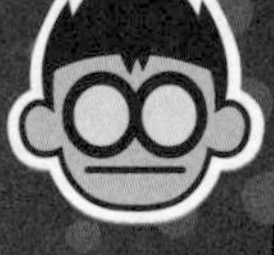

But you're right here. As *you*.

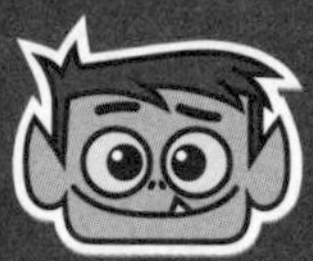

OMG WHAT IS HAPPENING AM I EVEN REAL?!

GREEN ARROW

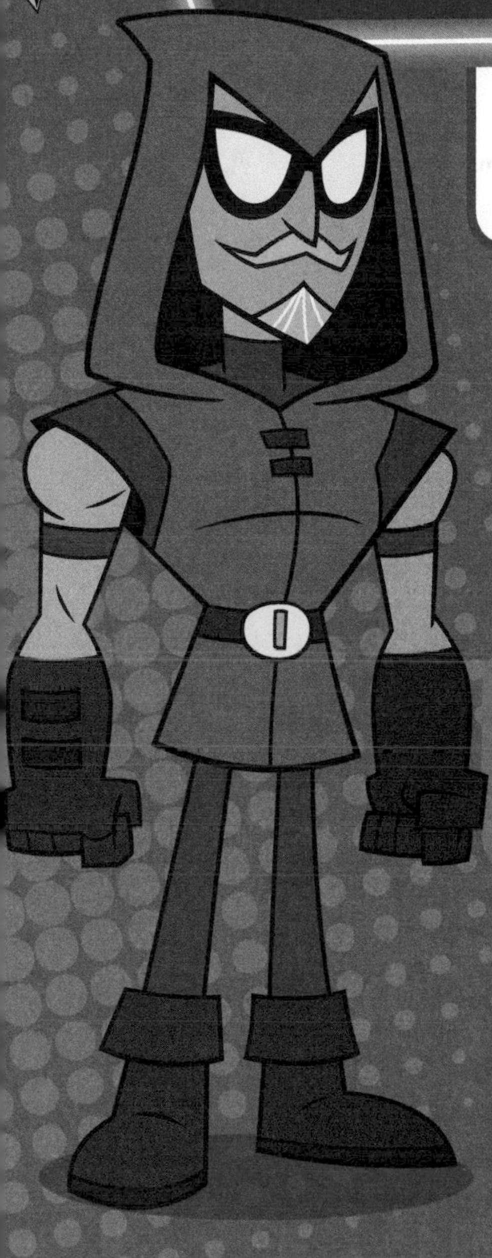

Real Name: Oliver Queen

Powers & Abilities: Master archer, skilled hand-to-hand fighter

And he's RICH.

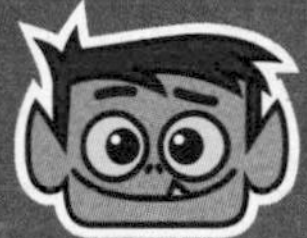

Money isn't everything, Beast Boy.

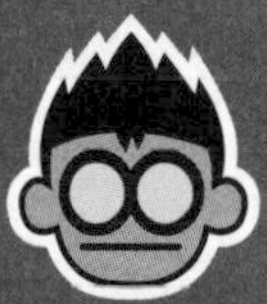

Says the guy who grew up in a ginormous mansion with a billionaire mentor who used his endless pockets to fund a war on crime.

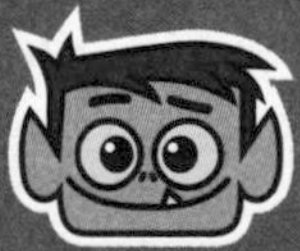

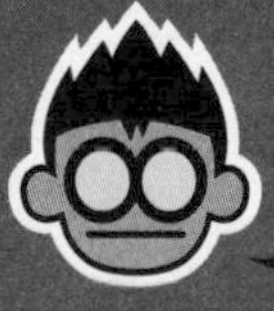

OMG WHAT IS HAPPENING AM I EVEN REAL?!

THE ATOM

Real Name: Ray Palmer

Powers & Abilities: Genius intellect, invented a size-changing belt, gets really little

Oh no! The Atom could get squished at any time!

Mmmhhhrrrmmhhhrrrrmmmmrrm.

What is he saying?! He is too small to understand.

I think...he's...using...the bathroom?

Oh. That is very unfortunate. But as a wise, spunky orphan once said, "When you gotta go, you gotta go!"

I never said that.

Different spunky orphan.

BATMAN

Real Name: REDACTED

Nicknames: Dark Knight, Caped Crusader

Powers & Abilities: Master detective, inventor, highly skilled martial artist, tactician

Batman's Likes: Playing guitar, hanging out with Jimmy "the Commish" Gordon, napping during the day, fishing, spying on the Teen Titans, watching his stories, creating a high-tech arsenal with which to fight crime because criminals are a superstitious and cowardly lot

And now the guy who scooped me up like a baby bird and gave my life purpose. My mentor (and stern father figure)...

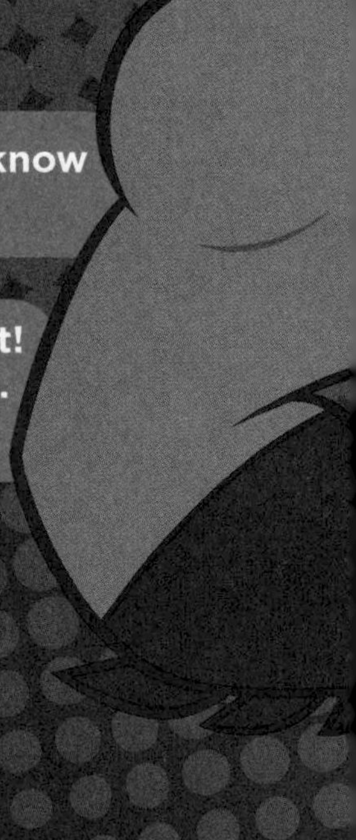

What the what?! Bro, we already know Batman's secret identity is REDACTED.

Hey! What's happening? Stop that! I can say REDACTED if I want to. REDACTED. REDACTED, REDACTED, REDACTED!

Sorry, but Batman's secret identity *must* remain a secret.

You mess with the Bat, you get the wing.

INSIDE THE BATCAVE

The Batcave is the ultimate crash pad. It's where Batman keeps the Batmobile, stashes all his snacks, and even keeps relics from past cases. Oh, and his giant flat-screen TV is pretty sweet, too. It's a great place to hang. That is, of course, if you're not afraid of bats pooping all over your stuff.

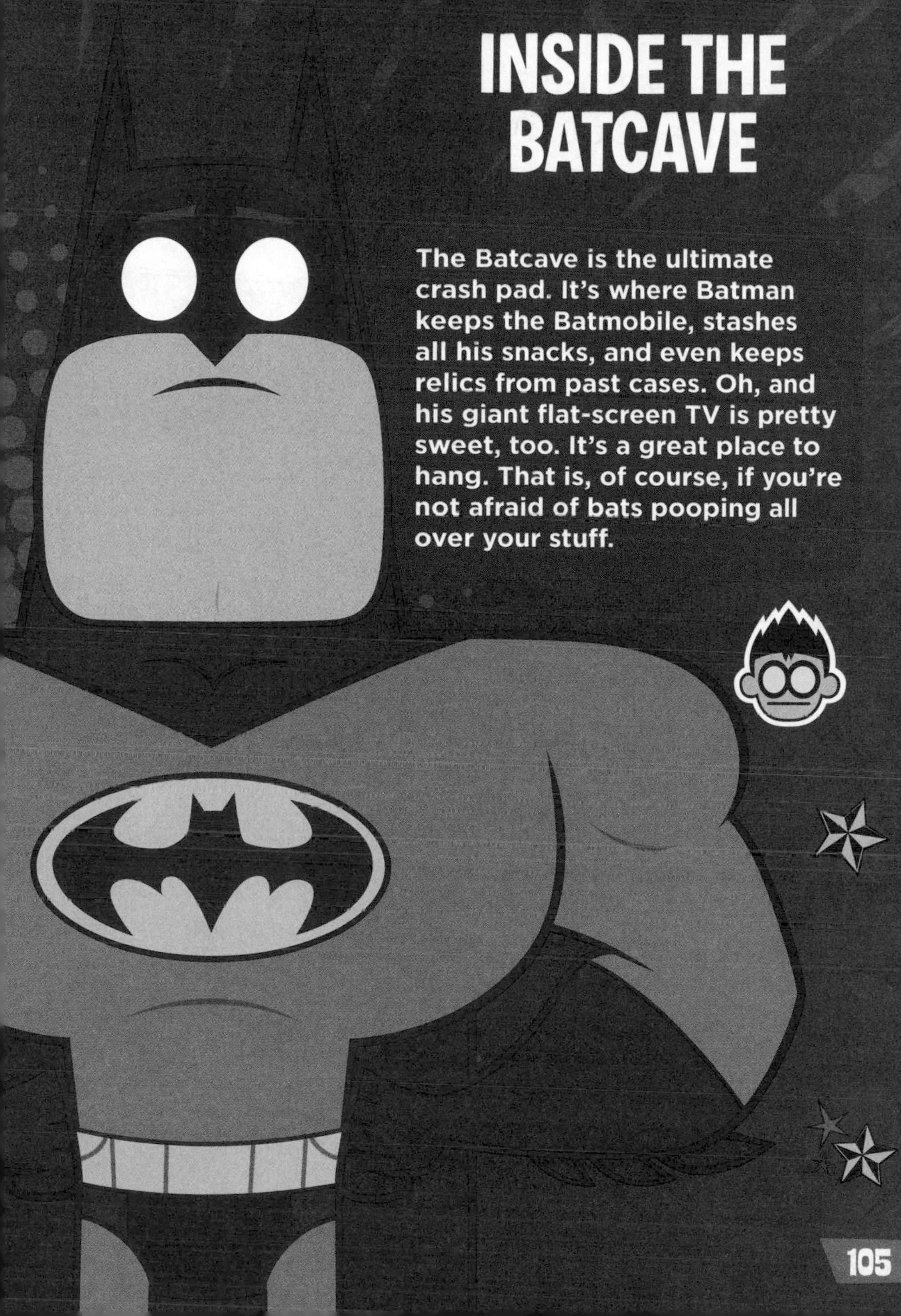

Ya-ha-ha-ha-ha! Don't forget about me! I am

BALLOON MAN,

scourge of the sky! Feel my airy wrath!

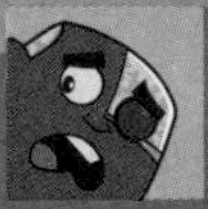

Didn't we defeat this dude once already?

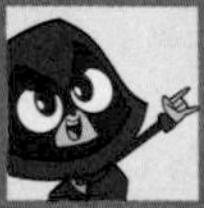

If there's anything I've learned in *this* business, it's that, defeat or no defeat, the windbags always come back.

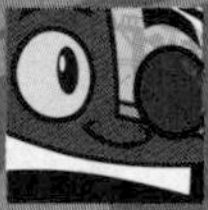

Not if you poke 'em in the butt!

DO NOT POKE ME IN THE BUTT.

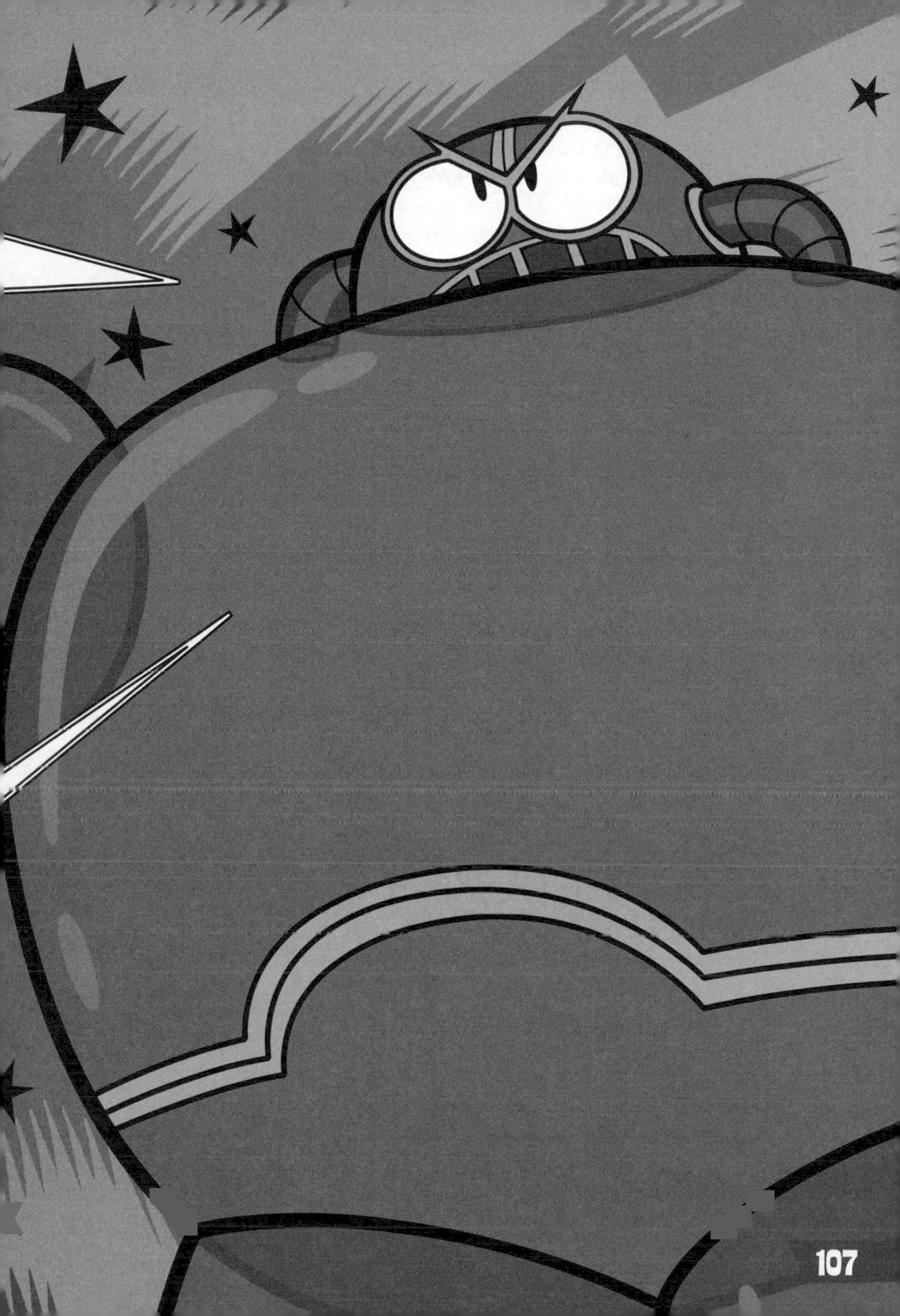

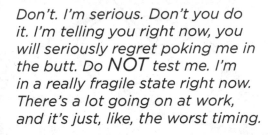

Don't. I'm serious. Don't you do it. I'm telling you right now, you will seriously regret poking me in the butt. Do NOT test me. I'm in a really fragile state right now. There's a lot going on at work, and it's just, like, the worst timing.

How about you cut ol' Balloon Man some slack, huh? HA! HA? "Cut me some slack"?!

I made a joke and I didn't even mean to. See? You don't want to poke a fellow goofster, now, do you?

Cy, poke him so we can move on.

Let the poking commence!

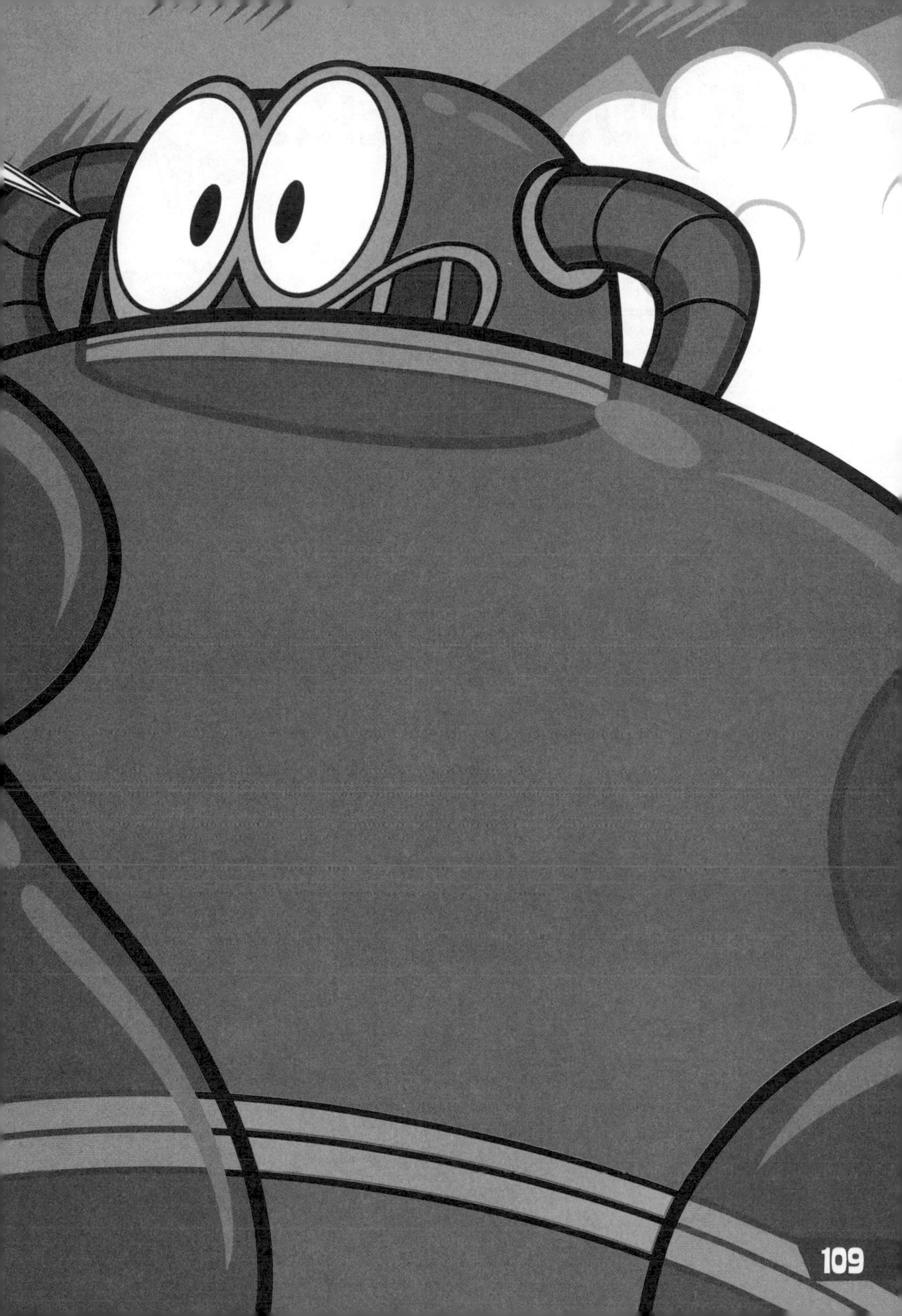

ONE POKE LATER...

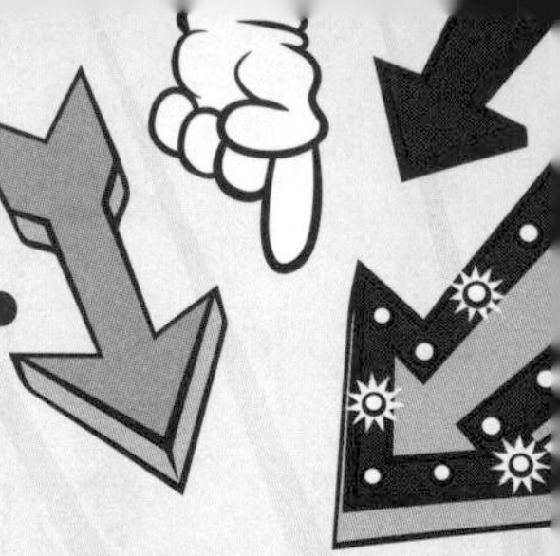

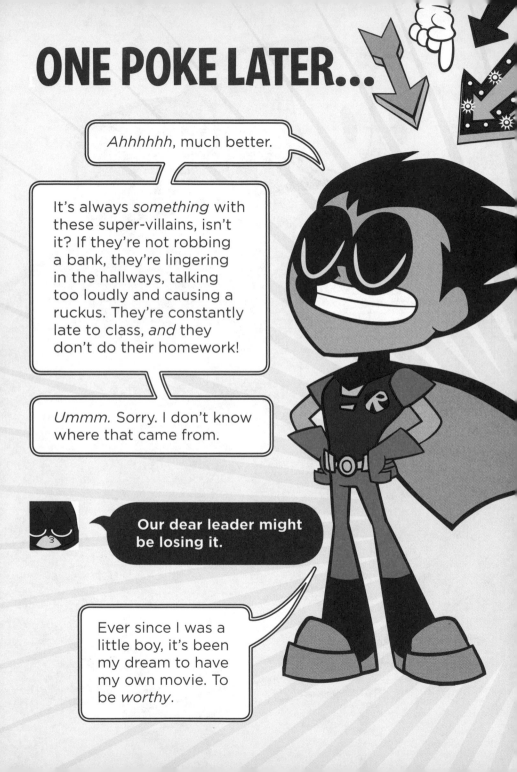

Ahhhhhh, much better.

It's always *something* with these super-villains, isn't it? If they're not robbing a bank, they're lingering in the hallways, talking too loudly and causing a ruckus. They're constantly late to class, *and* they don't do their homework!

Ummm. Sorry. I don't know where that came from.

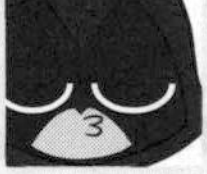

Our dear leader might be losing it.

Ever since I was a little boy, it's been my dream to have my own movie. To be *worthy*.

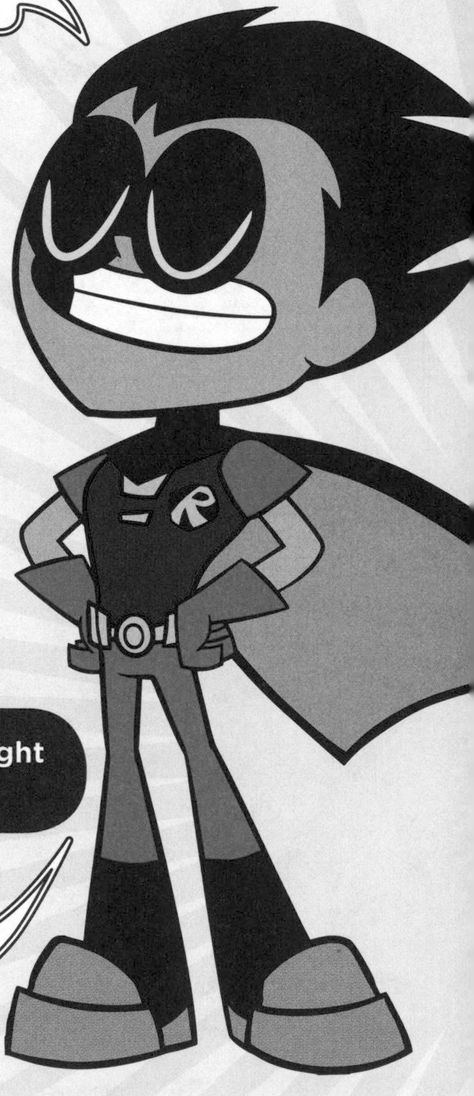

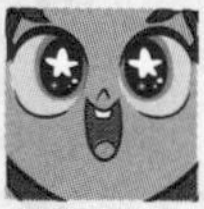

But you *are* worthy, Robin!

Thanks, Starfire.

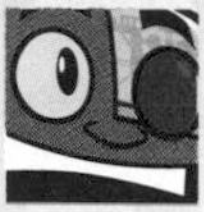

And you were a boy basically a second ago.

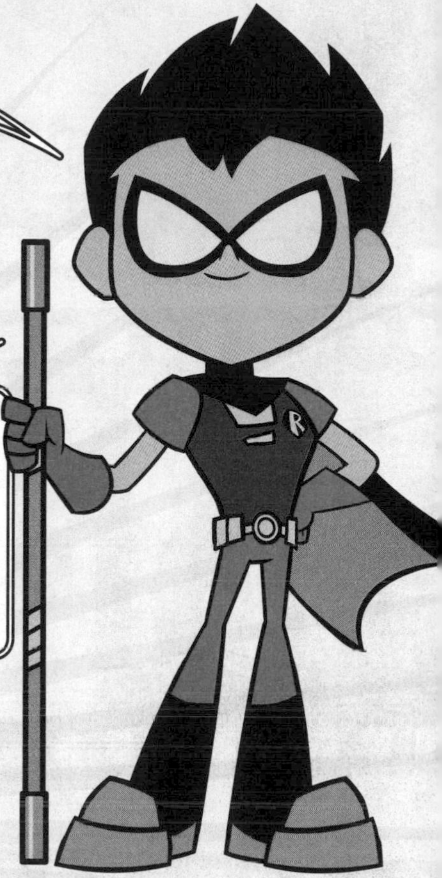

See? This is what I'm talking about! Sidekicks don't get the respect they deserve. I've put my time in. I've vacuumed the Batmobile. I've polished the Batarangs. Robin deserves to be taken seriously!

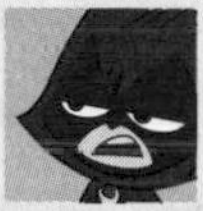

There's that third person again.

Being the star of my very own super hero movie would cement my status as more than just some handsome, charming acrobat. I'd be a contender. At last! But, things don't alwasy go as planned. Super hero movies might be super, crazy popular, but it's not like they just give them to *anyone*.

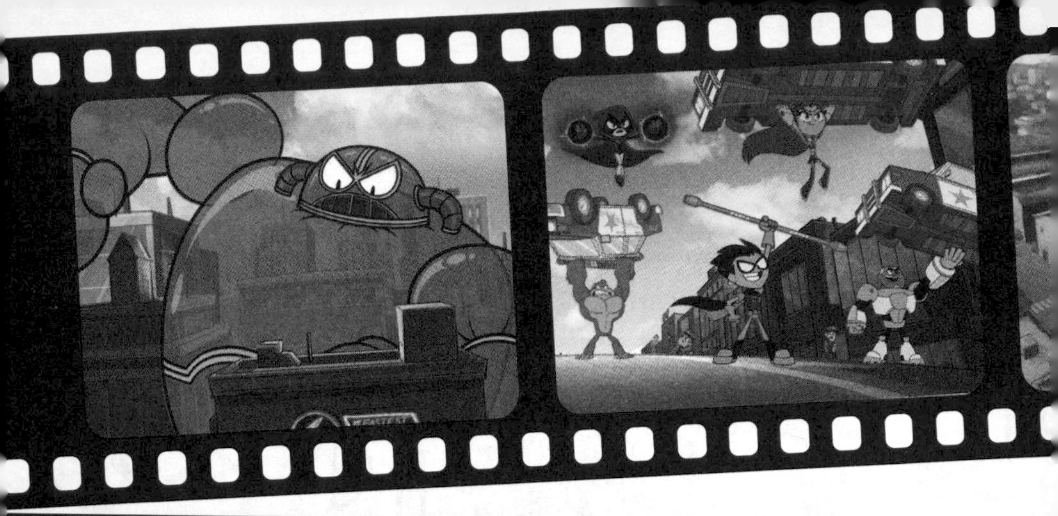

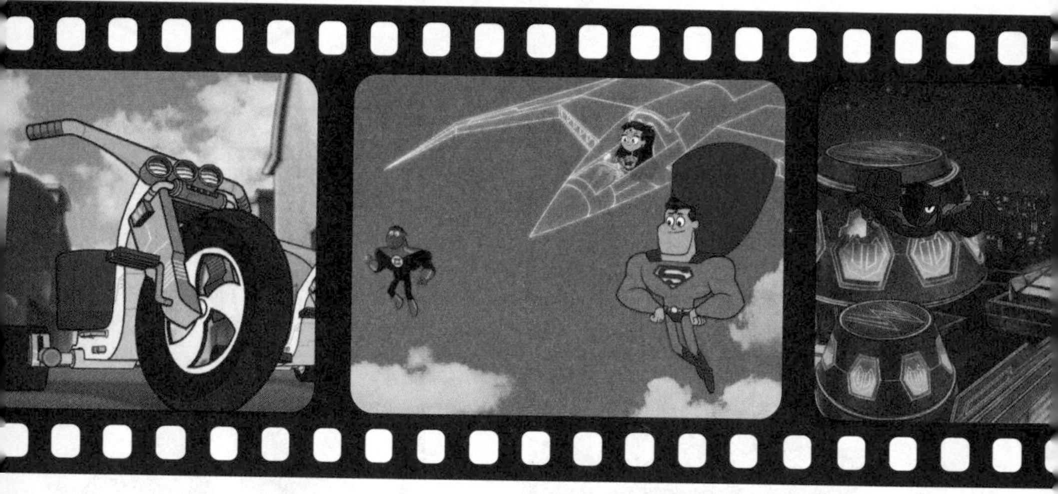

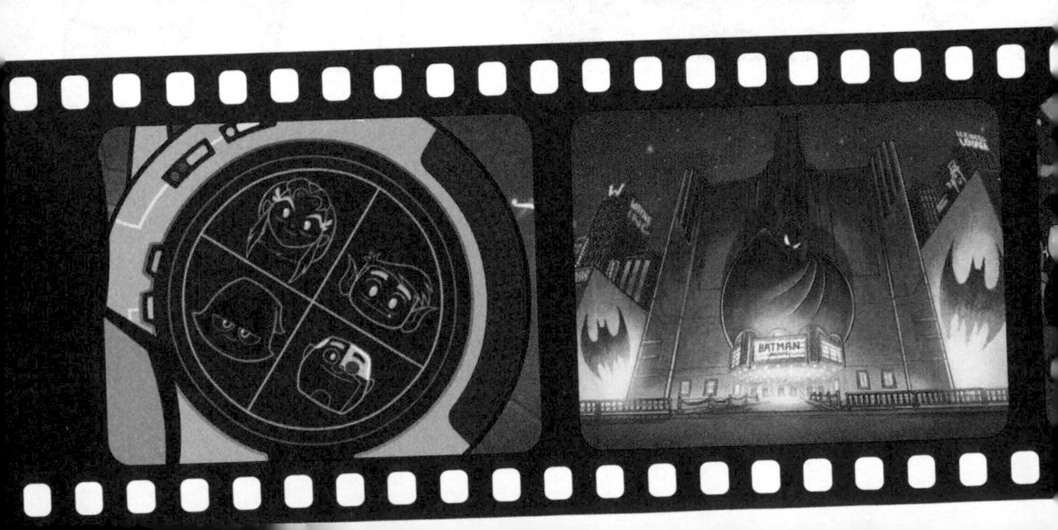
BATMAN

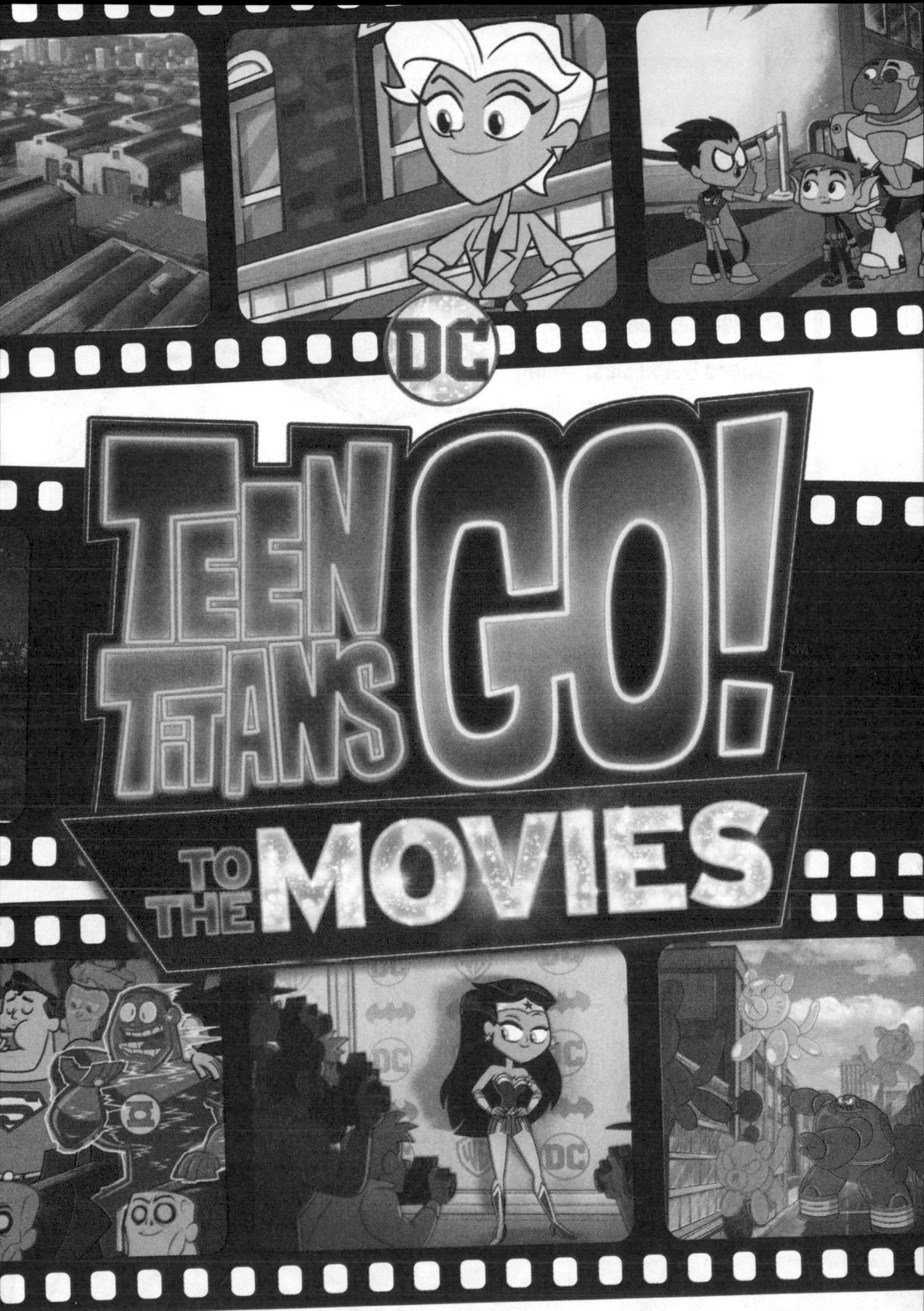
DC
TEEN TITANS GO!
TO THE MOVIES

JADE WILSON

FAMOUS HOLLYWOOD DIRECTOR

Real Name: Jade Wilson

Powers & Abilities: Ability to manage a large-scale film budget without losing her mind

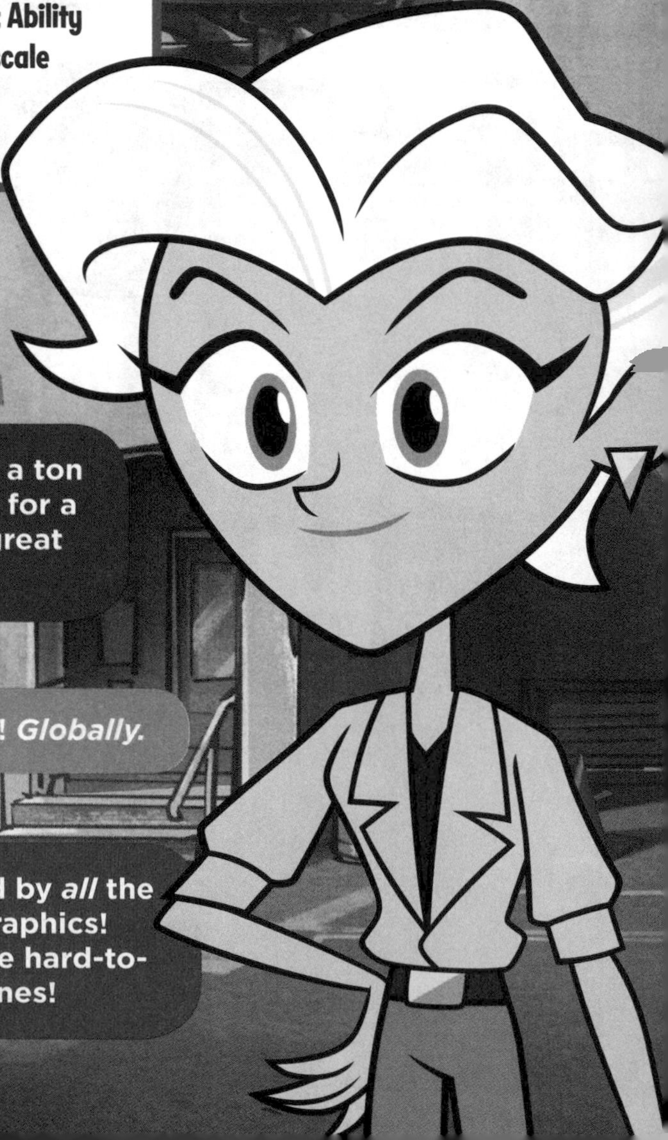

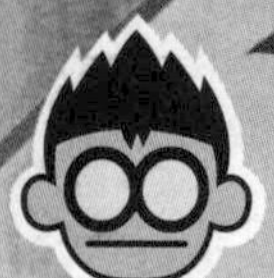

She did a ton of work for a ton of great movies.

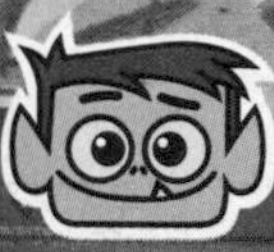

Big hits! *Globally.*

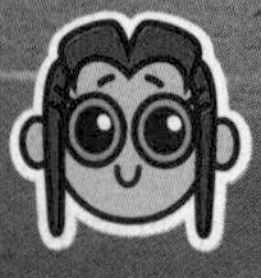

Beloved by *all* the demographics! Even the hard-to-reach ones!

I couldn't have said it better myself, Starfire. JADE WILSON FOREVER! When I asked Jade about making a movie for us, she had all kinds of good advice to share....

JADE WILSON'S WORDS OF WISDOM

"Quiet on the set!"

"Get out of the business."

"Action!"

"Are there any more of those chocolate-covered peanuts at the craft service table? Could someone bring me some chocolate-covered peanuts, please?"

"Cut!"

"The only way I'd EVER consider making a movie about the Teen Titans is if they were the only super heroes left in the universe!"

That last one was rough to hear. But! It also gave me a big idea. What if there was a way to make it so the Teen Titans *were* the only super heroes left in the universe? I knew that accomplishing a task like that wouldn't be easy. We'd need to show diligence and precision if we were going to change the face of HISTORY.

What does history's face look like?

YO MAMA, Mama.

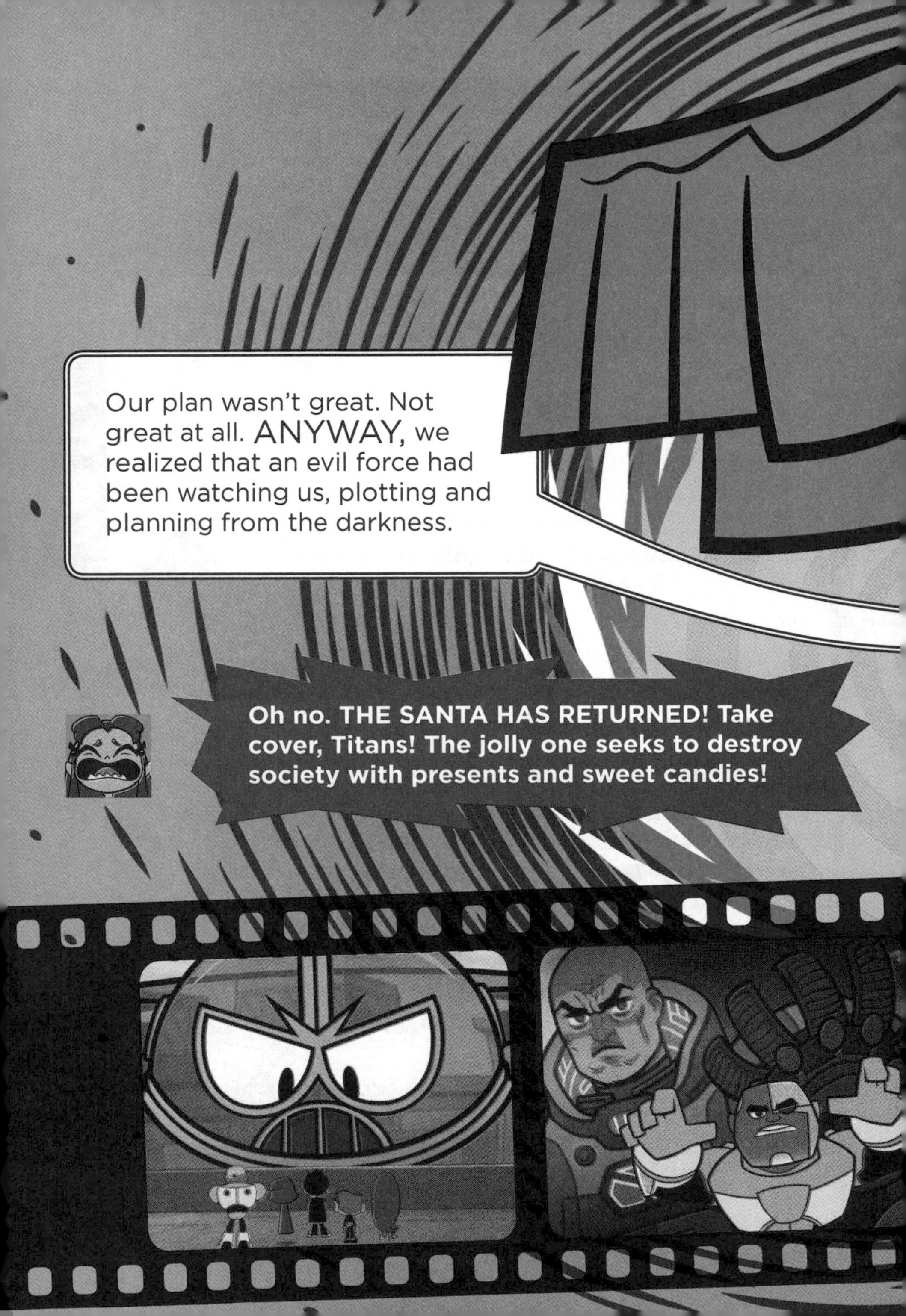
Our plan wasn't great. Not great at all. ANYWAY, we realized that an evil force had been watching us, plotting and planning from the darkness.
Oh no. THE SANTA HAS RETURNED! Take cover, Titans! The jolly one seeks to destroy society with presents and sweet candies!

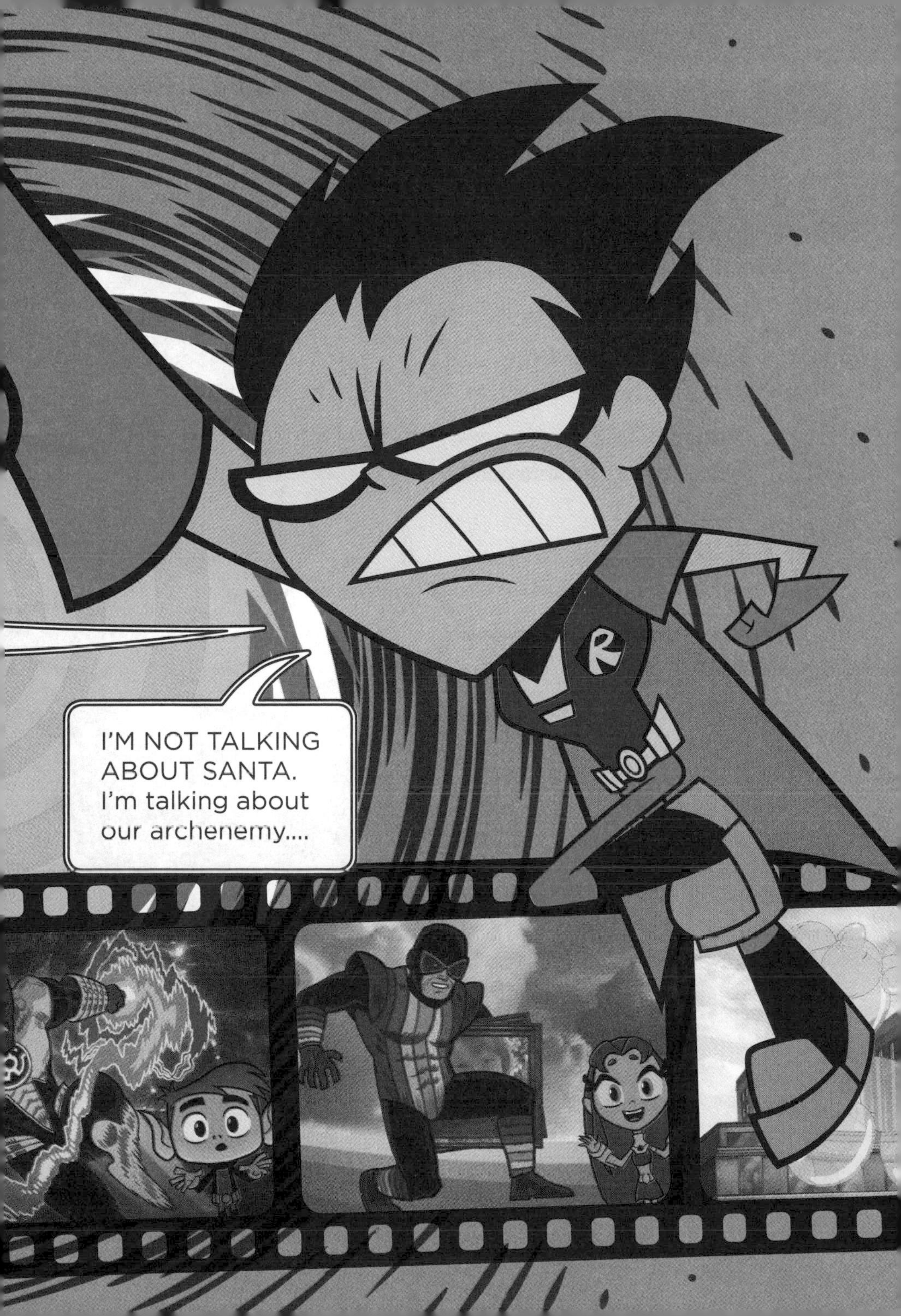
I'M NOT TALKING ABOUT SANTA. I'm talking about our archenemy....

SLADE

Real Name: Slade

Nicknames: Deathstroke the Terminator

Powers & Abilities: Weapons master, superb hand-to-hand combatant

Archnemesis: THE TEEN TITANS, SILLY!

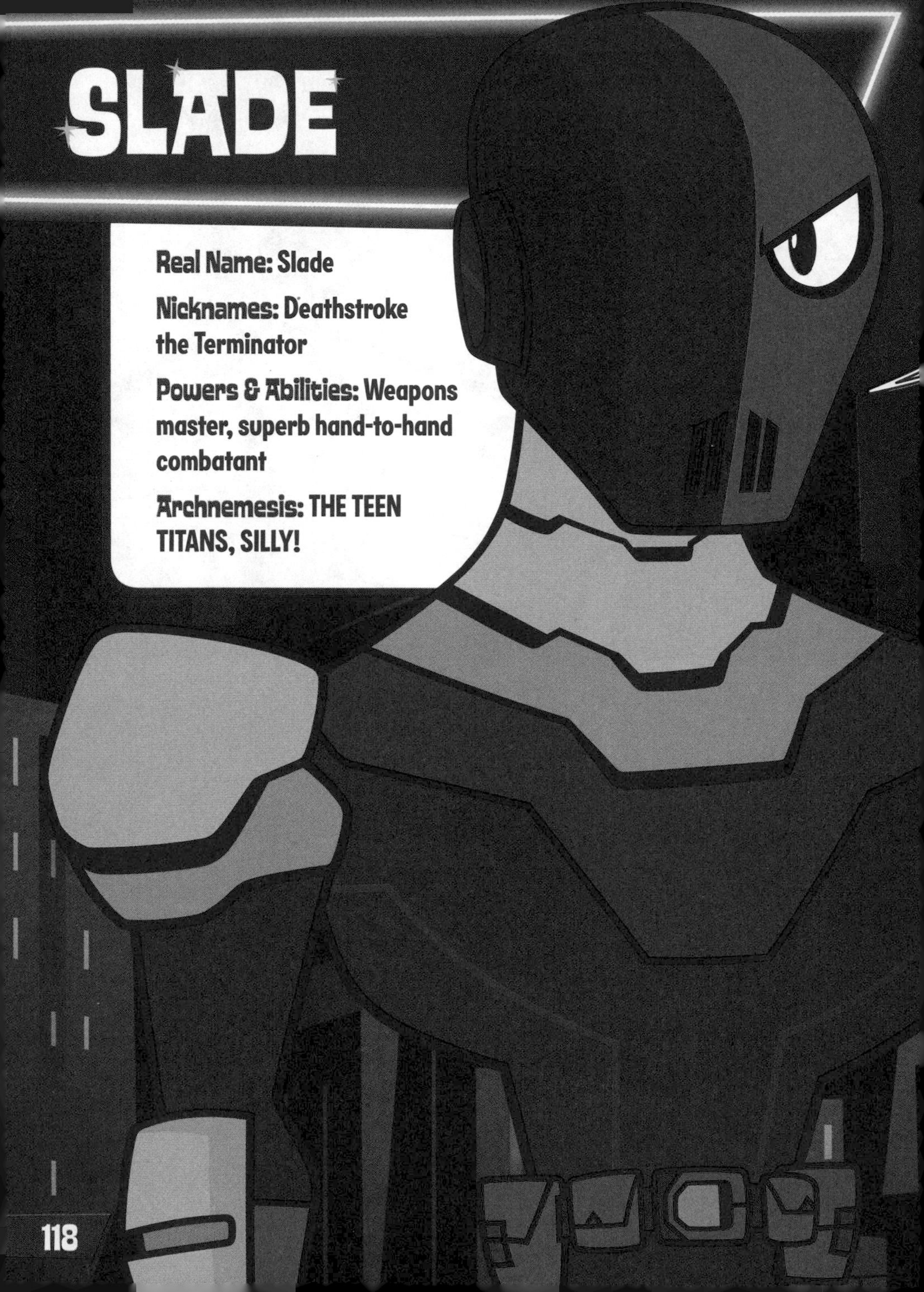

In my spare time, I enjoy analyzing personal dynamics in order to create psychological profiles of my enemies that allow me to manipulate minds through visual trickery and incessant cajoling.

Some people have called him the *greatest super-villain the world has ever seen.*

And by "some people," I mean him. He called himself that. But it doesn't matter who said it, because it's true. Slade's been a thorn in the Teen Titans' side for a long time.

Slade is *baaaaaad* news.

Slade uses all kinds of nasty weapons like swords and smoke bombs. And when he runs out of that stuff, dude'll use a chicken leg to whop people in the butt. YA HEARD. He mean.

Slade has a lot of dirty tricks up his sleeve, including the classic "You've got something on your shirt!" and the timeless "What's that behind you?" techniques.

After a fierce battle with Slade, we tossed him in jail, and justice reigned supreme once again!

Dude. That's a bold lie. He escaped.

Yeah, I know. He does that. But the good news was that my quest for validation took a turn for the exciting.

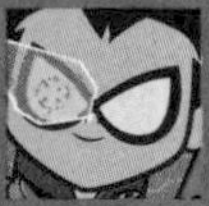

Then a whole bunch of incredibly epic stuff happened.

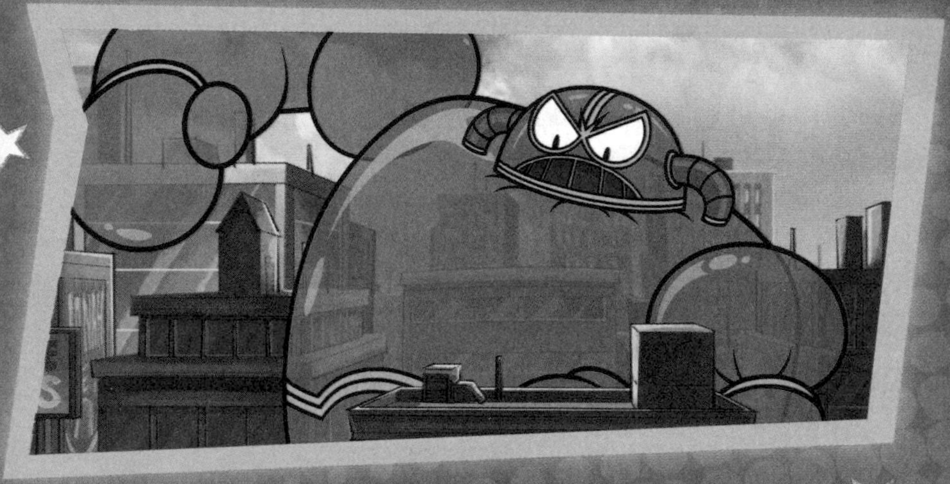

First, Balloon Man attacked.

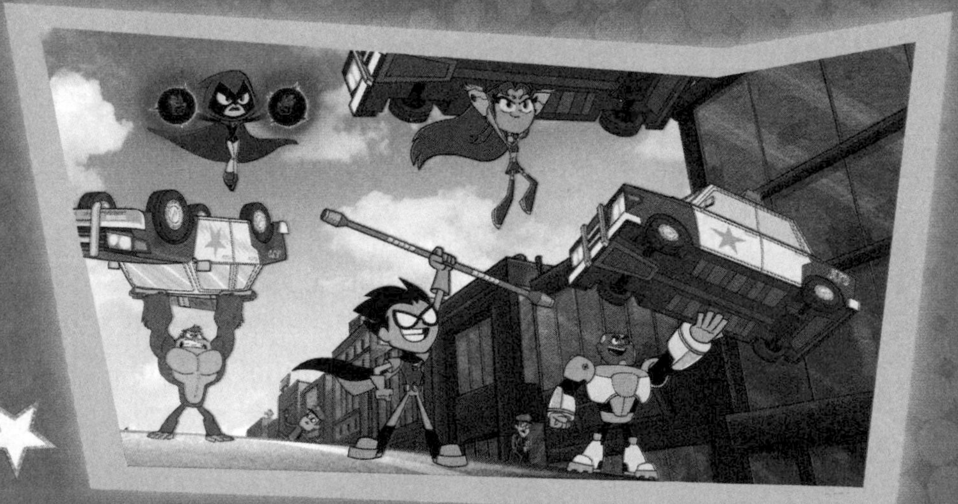

But it was cool—the Teen Titans are the bravest heroes around!

But also, Balloon Man didn't care about that all too much.

The Justice League arrived to help!

It really got out of hand.

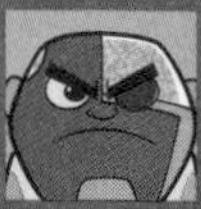

YEAH, BOY! Everyone was running and yelling and crying.

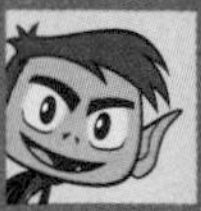

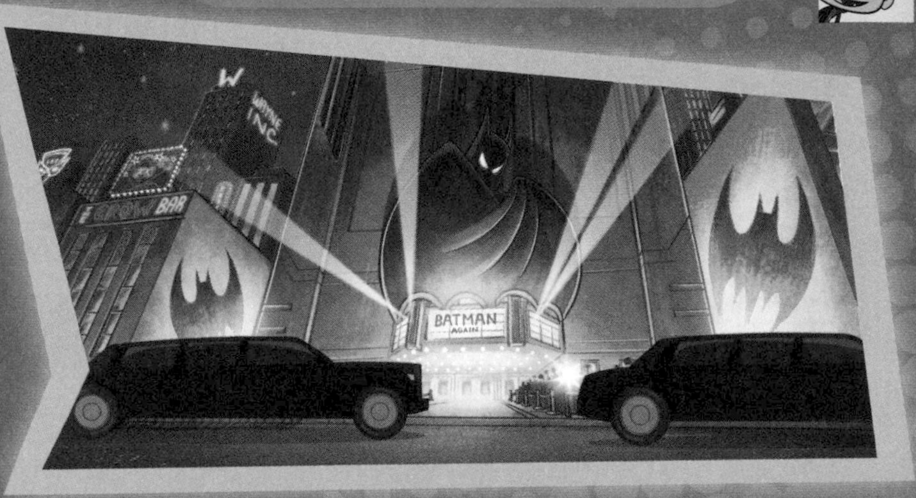
BATMAN
AGAIN

The Titans got to see the new Batman movie. But then they realized that they'd been overlooked for their own movie.

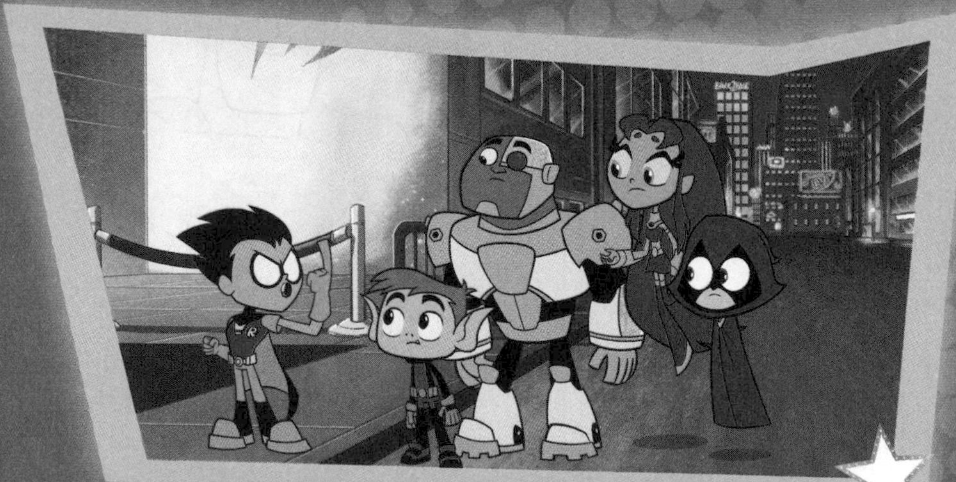

You were the only one crying.

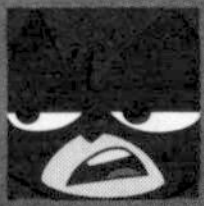

AND ROBIN! DO NOT FORGET THE ROBIN CRYING!

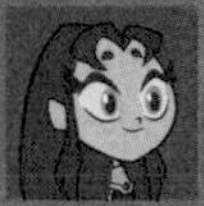

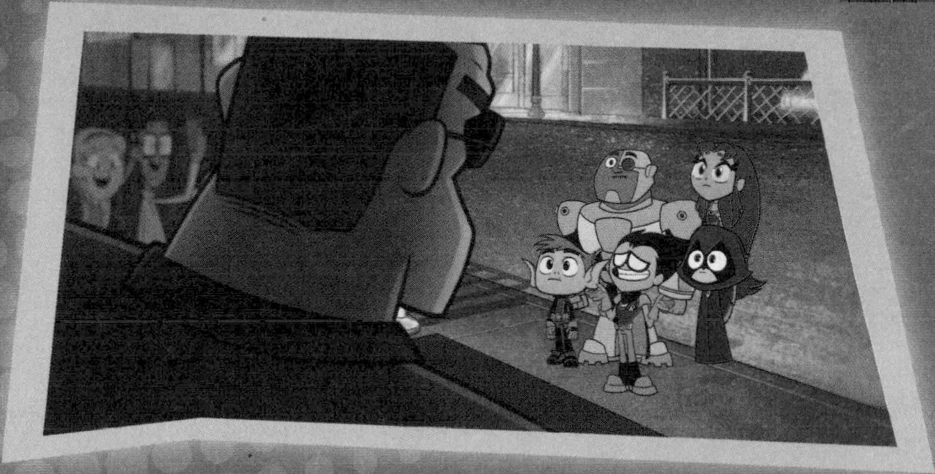

Nobody was taking them seriously. In the meantime, a new villain burst on the scene.

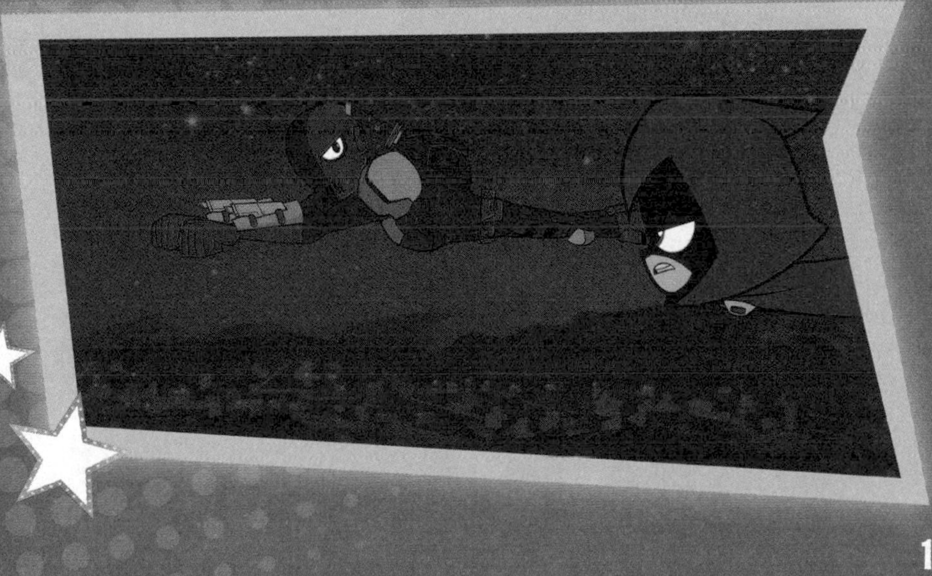

There were just so many emotions flying around all willy-nilly.

Things. Got

And portals. You needed so many portals in order to move the action.

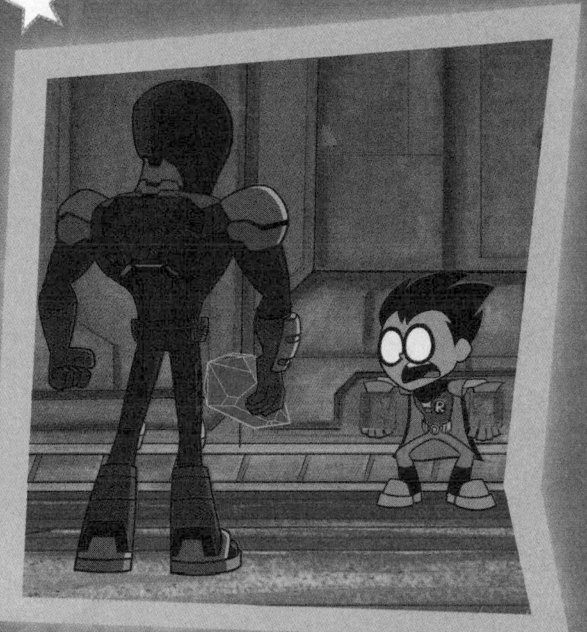

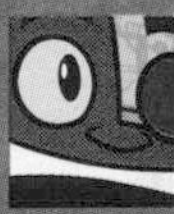

Oh, and bad decision-making. Robin made a LOT of bad decisions.

Mega. Intense.

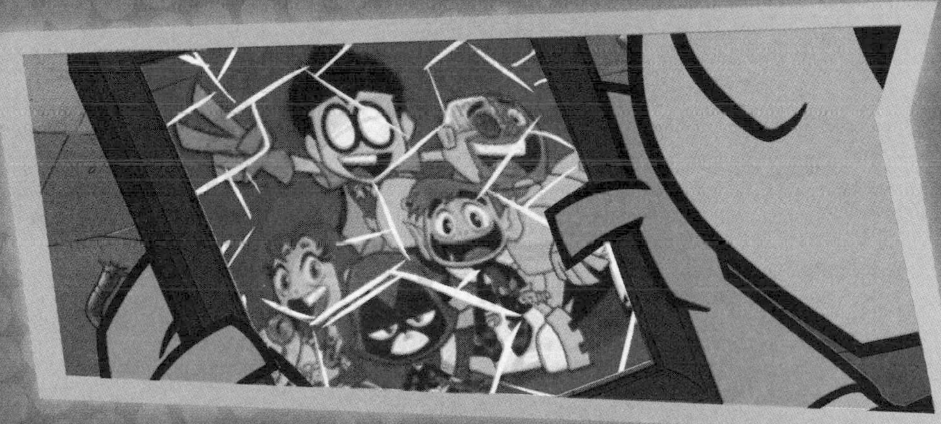

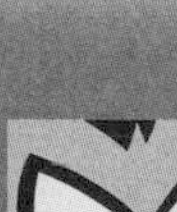

You guys, you're missing the point! We were so close! We were so dramatic! There was an opportunity for an actual archvillain running around! He wanted to take over the world!

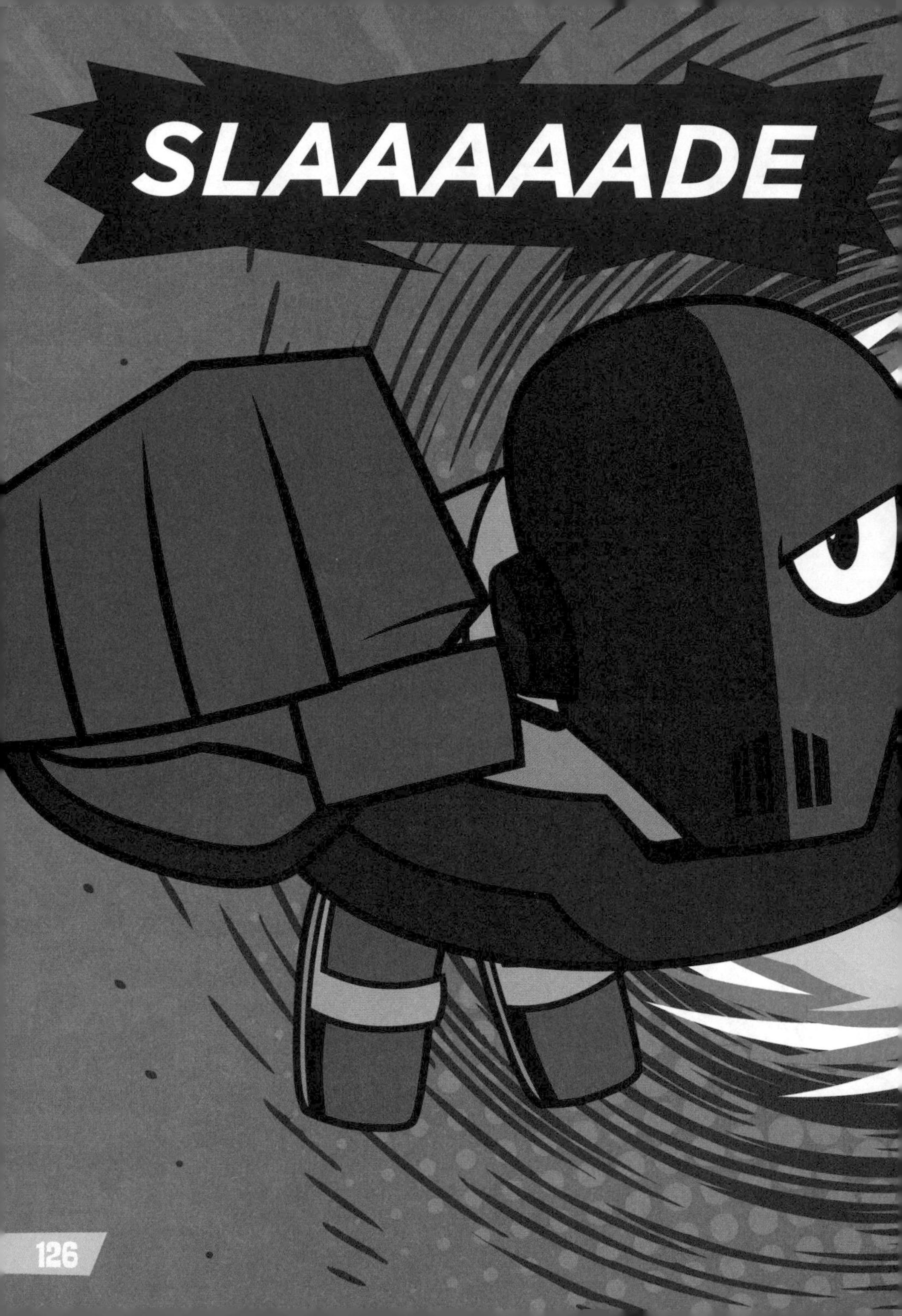
SLAAAAADE

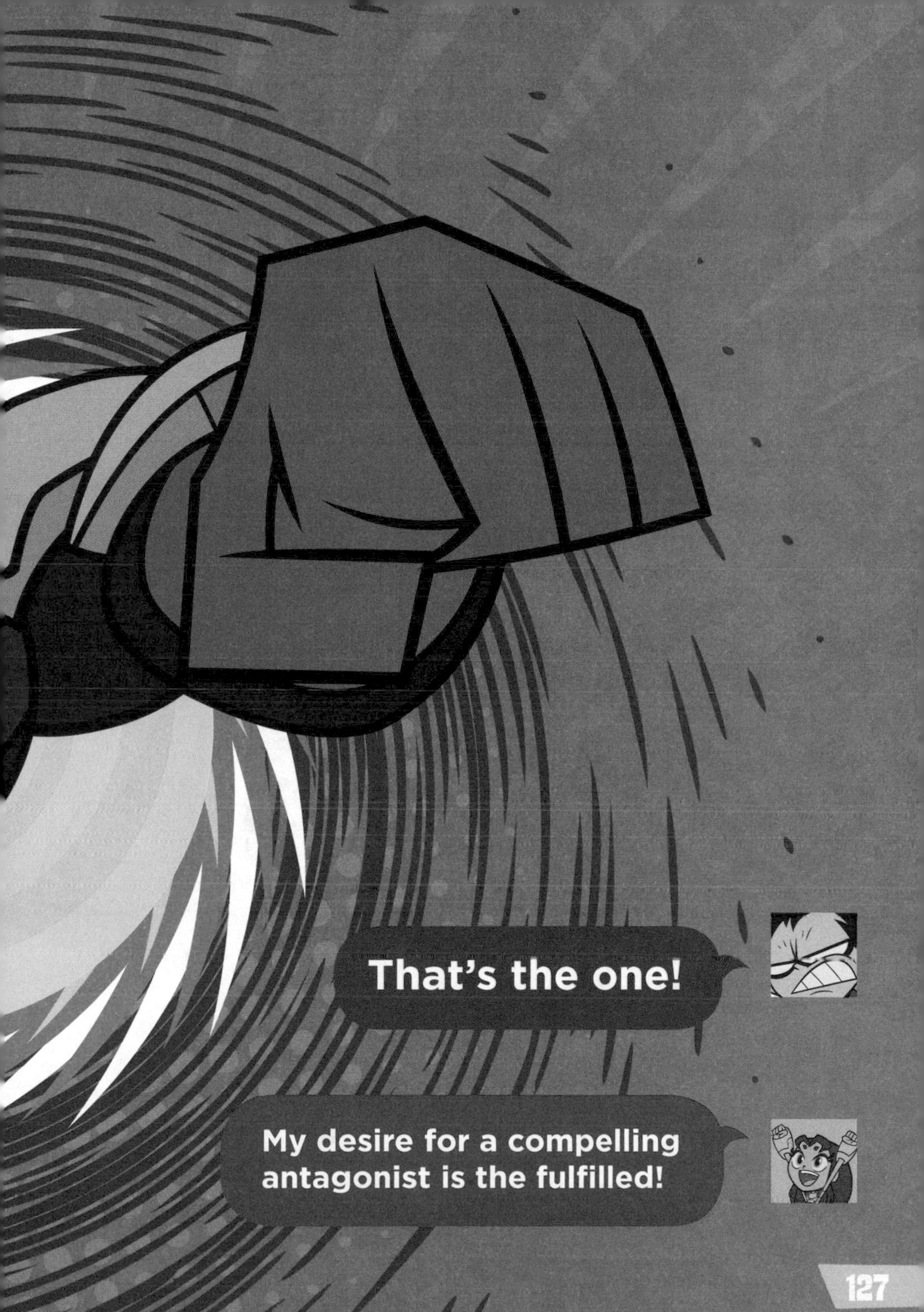
That's the one!
My desire for a compelling antagonist is the fulfilled!

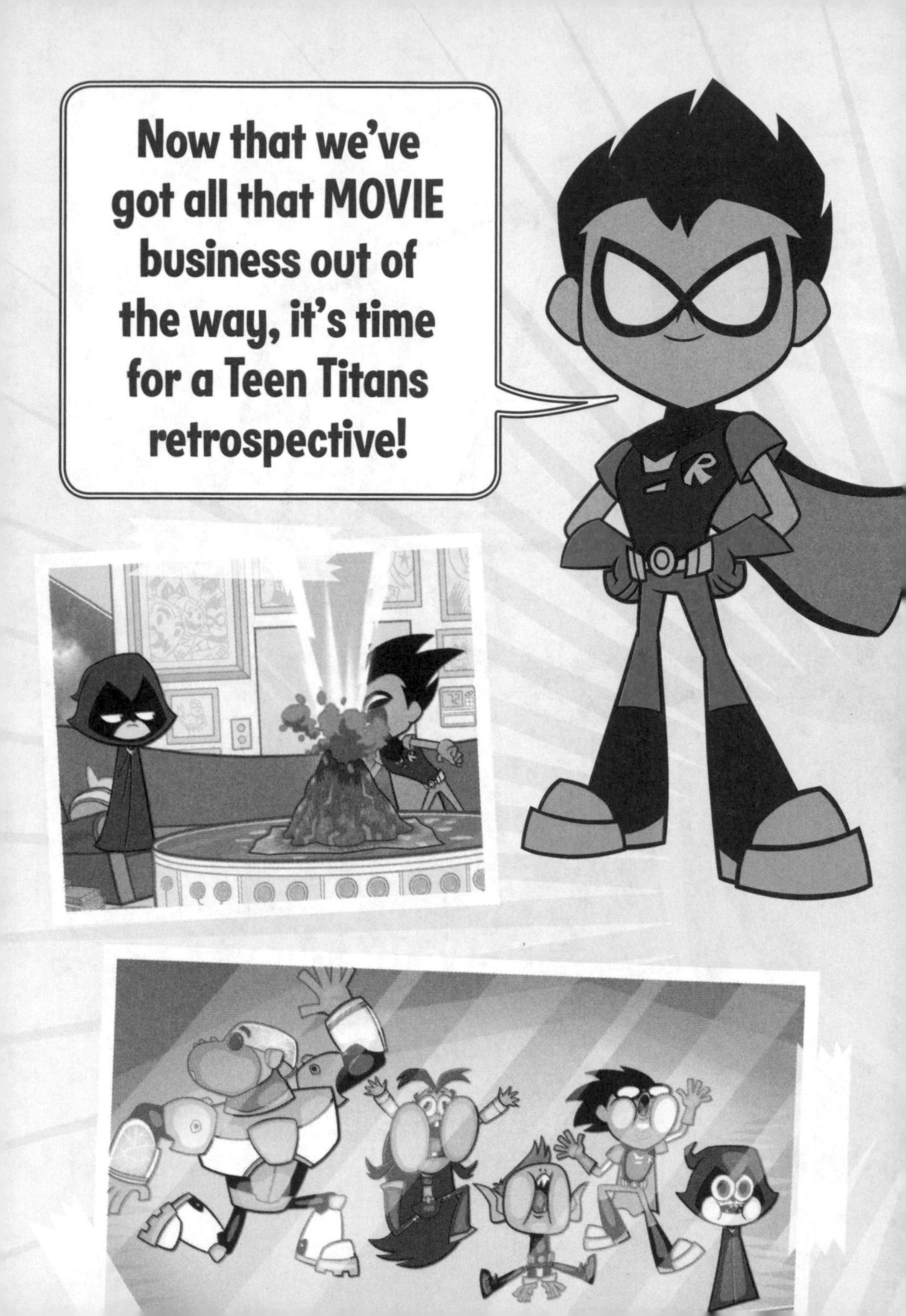
Now that we've got all that MOVIE business out of the way, it's time for a Teen Titans retrospective!

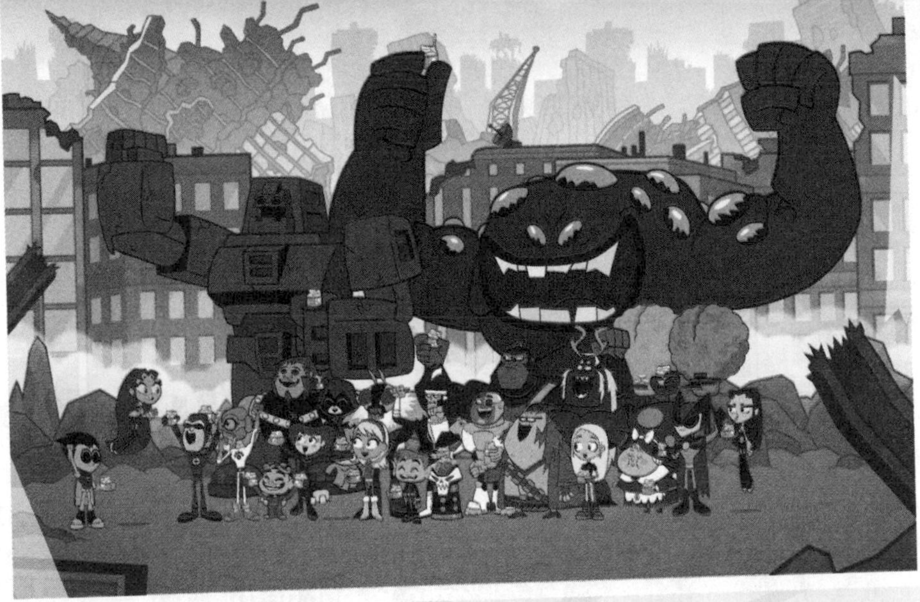
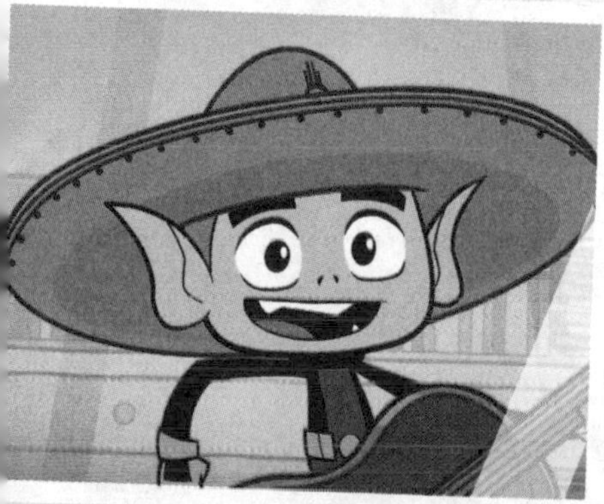
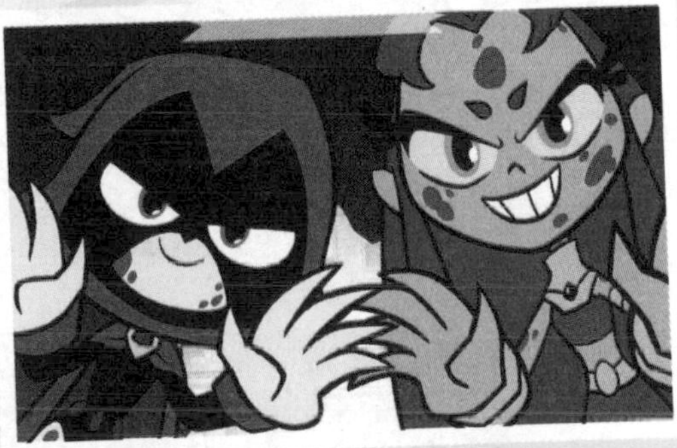
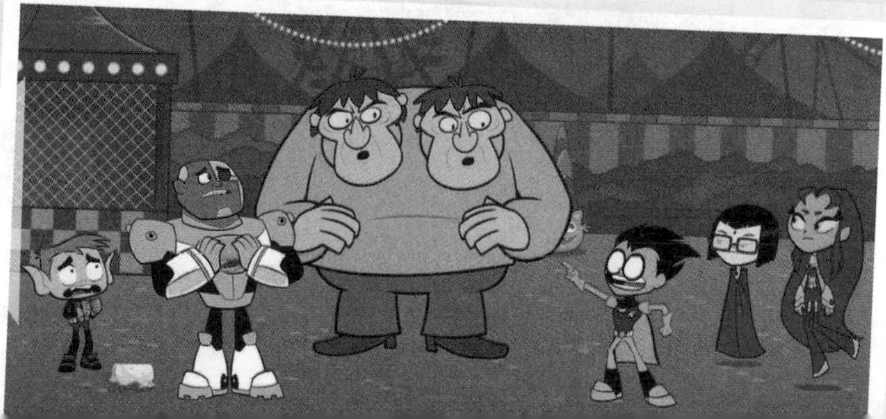

Journeying through the past is how you inspire yourself to be better in the future! As long as you do not *dwell* on the mistakes of yesterday. That would not be the good idea. It can often lead to a spiral into the darkness.

Tell me about it.

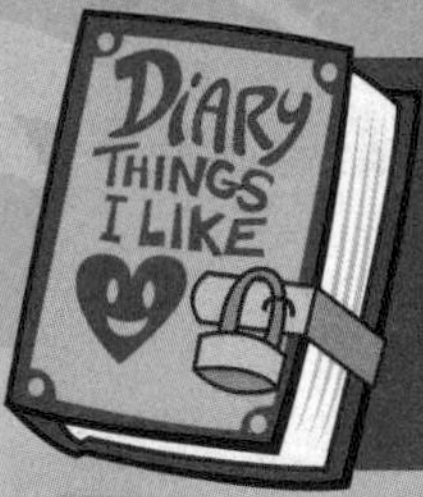
DIARY
THINGS
I LIKE

I wish to show you all how far the Teen Titans have come in our heroic odyssey. Let us glimpse our former selves and acknowledge our growth.

You know what, Starfire? I think that's a great idea.

I do, too, Robin.
That is why I just suggested it.

My old notebook?! Uh, where did you find this?

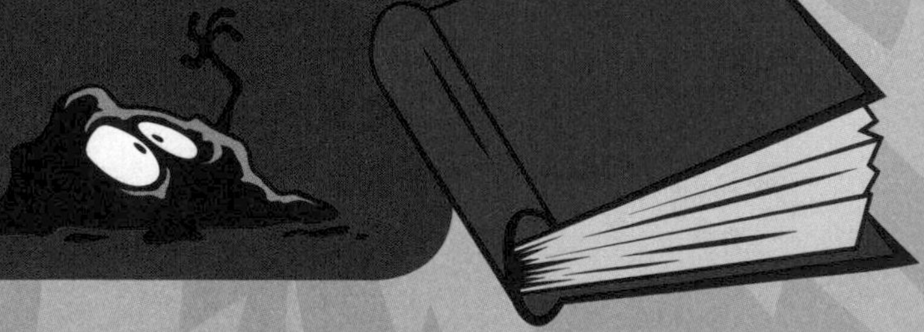

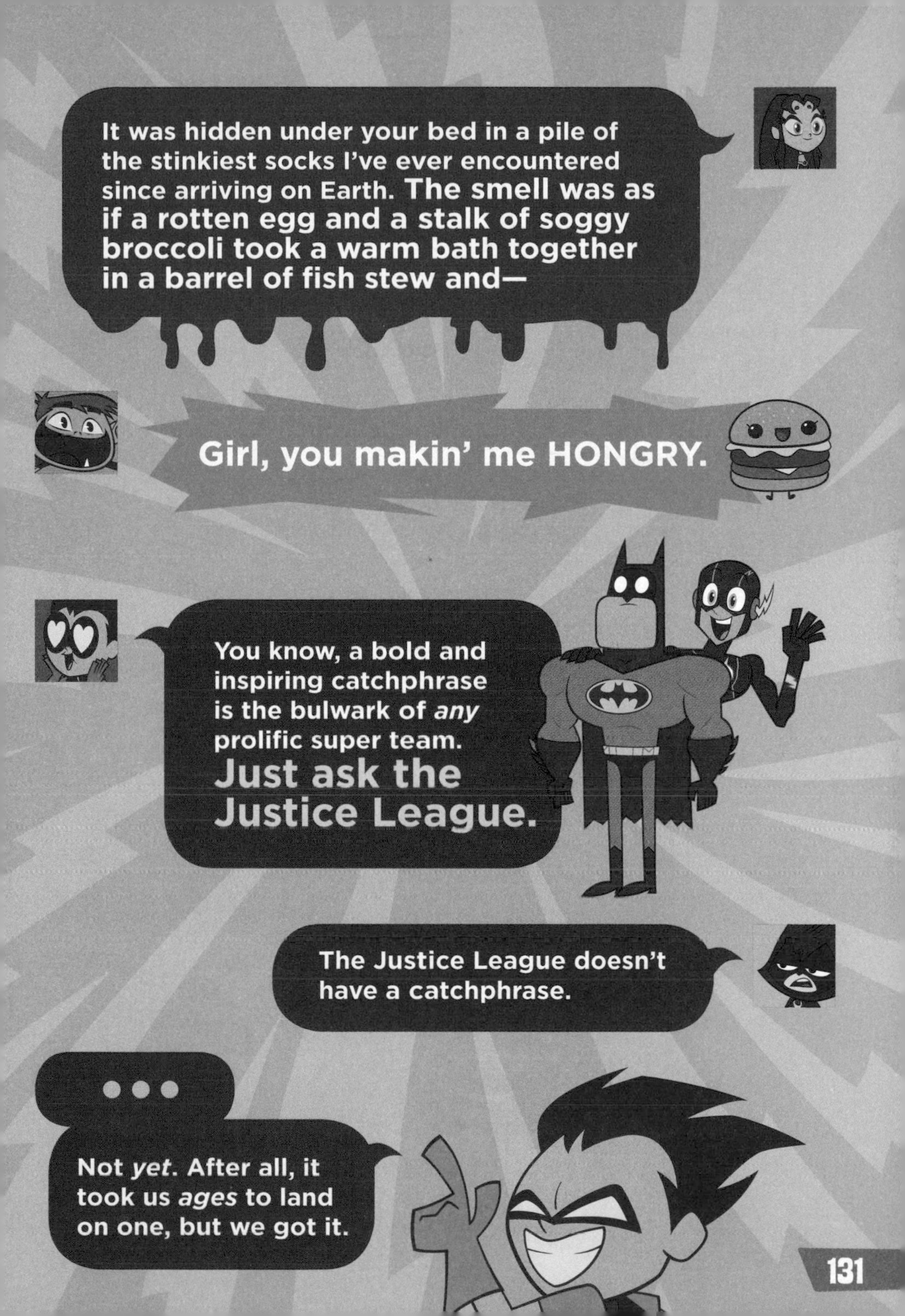
It was hidden under your bed in a pile of the stinkiest socks I've ever encountered since arriving on Earth. The smell was as if a rotten egg and a stalk of soggy broccoli took a warm bath together in a barrel of fish stew and—
Girl, you makin' me HONGRY.
You know, a bold and inspiring catchphrase is the bulwark of *any* prolific super team. Just ask the Justice League.
The Justice League doesn't have a catchphrase.
• • •
Not *yet*. After all, it took us *ages* to land on one, but we got it.

REJECTED TITANS CATCHPHRASES

Titans, NOW!

Go, go, Titans!

Titans, EAT TACOS!

Awww, what's the matter? Does baby need...THE TITANS?

MOVE IT! TITANS COMIN' THROUGH!

Let's go Titan-ing.

~~Can you smell what the Titans are cookin'~~?

Titans, let's get WOKE.

Excuse me! Someone is trying to TITAN in here!

TITANS SMASH.

~~TITANS! GITCHIA TITANS HEEEAH~~!

Hello. We're the Teen Titans. Need saving?

~~Who dem Titans? WE DEM TITANS~~.

~~There's always time for a Titan.~~

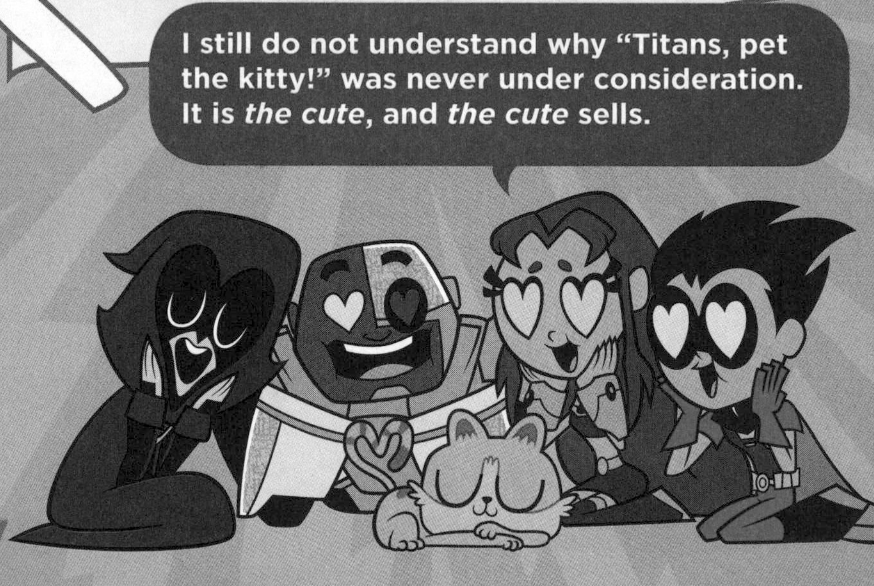
I still do not understand why "Titans, pet the kitty!" was never under consideration. It is *the cute*, and *the cute* sells.

We've come a long way!

I need a minute to take this all in. These photos are *a lot* to process. I need a lot of minutes.

BABY HANDS!

Nothing made me feel more alive than that infinity scarf.

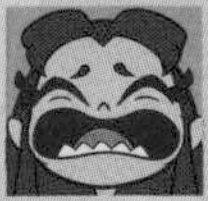

Do not break your toys. It will give you the nightmares.

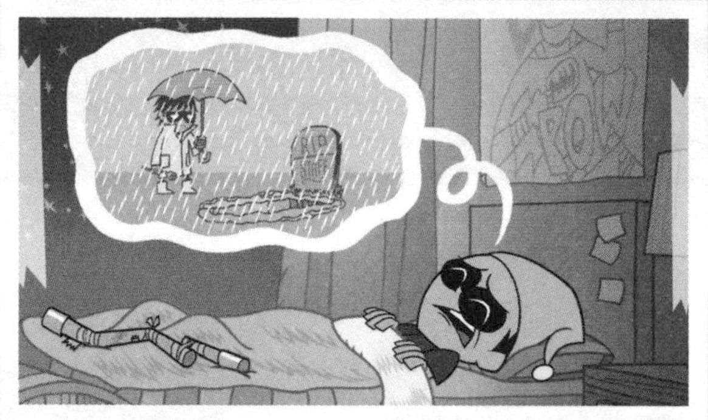

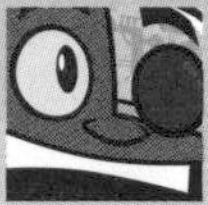

I feel RAD just looking at this.

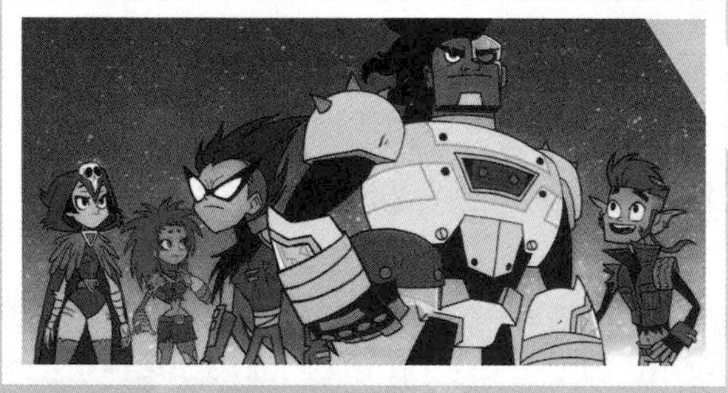

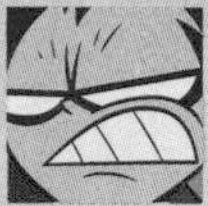

Ugh. That's depressing.

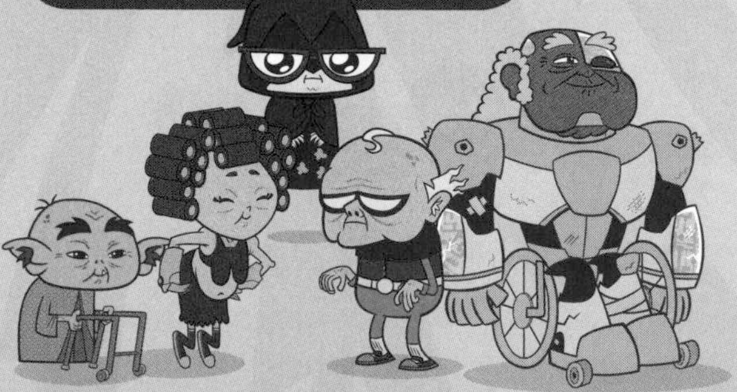

Reading these sweet messages makes my heart burst into **a million tiny hearts**! Then those hearts melt into a river of nectar, which re-forms into a new, bigger heart that replaces the original. It is the complicated *and* the simple.

What she said.

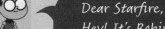

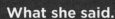

Dear Starfire,

Hey! It's Robin. We're friends from work. Ha-ha-ha. Remember? That's a line from our favorite movie, Friends from Work, in case you forgot. Sooo anyway, we fought Jinx today and she zapped me with a truth spell, so I thought I would take this opportunity to tell you you're pretty dang amazing. I see your soul. <u>I SEE IT</u>. Your soul radiates kindness. Your eyes are like pools...of...eyes. Wait. That's not what I meant to say. This spell is making me feel funky and not the way Beast Boy feels funky after too many burritos. Oh well, um, thanks for being a beacon of light in a dark world.

-Robin

STARFIRE, THIS NOTE WAS SUPPOSED TO BE PRIVATE!

Oh, Robin, do not be ashamed of your words. They are the purest of pure.

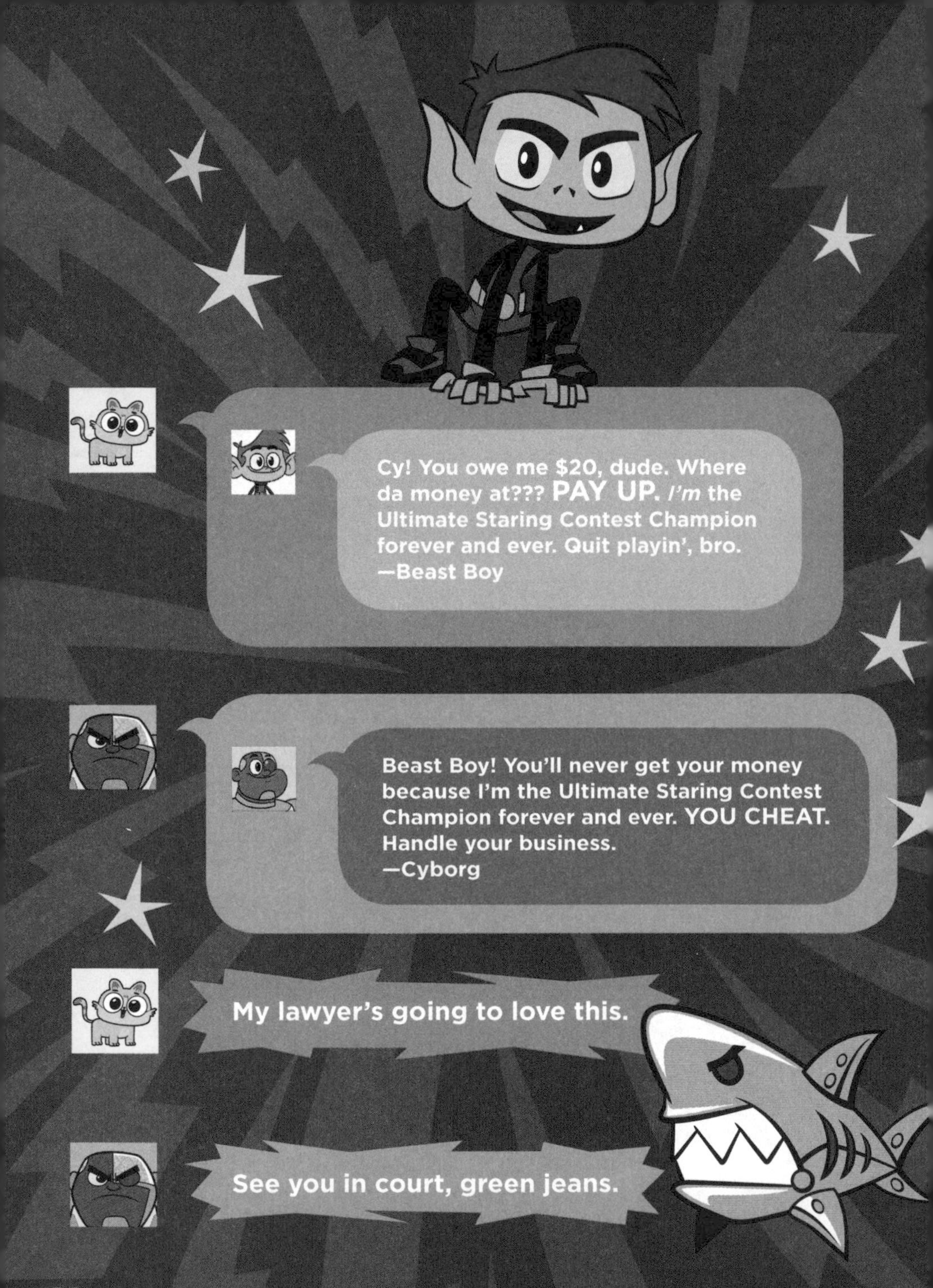
Cy! You owe me $20, dude. Where da money at??? PAY UP. *I'm* the Ultimate Staring Contest Champion forever and ever. Quit playin', bro.
—Beast Boy
Beast Boy! You'll never get your money because I'm the Ultimate Staring Contest Champion forever and ever. YOU CHEAT. Handle your business.
—Cyborg
My lawyer's going to love this.
See you in court, green jeans.

Raven—
It's me, *you. Oh, hey, what's up, girl?* Nothing much. *How are you?* Good, good. Working on my soul-self as usual. *You still with the Teen Titans?* Yeah, they're cool. *NOICE.* Let's hang out soon. *That would be really great.* Hit me up at the Tower. *I will totes do that.*
—Raven

I can explain....

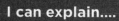

Actually, no. I'm not going to explain that. I'm an enigma, and enigmas don't explain things.

I was bored.

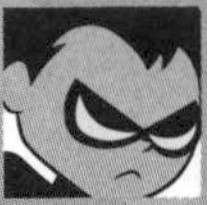

Okay. That's enough strolling down memory lane. I did what I came here to do, and now it's time to wrap this whole thing up. The Teen Titans are an incredible crime-fighting force for good that's come a long way since their early days, blah blah blah.

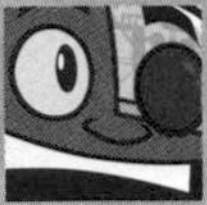

We had some laughs. We had some cries.

When did you *cry*, Cyborg?

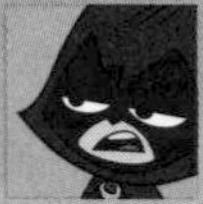

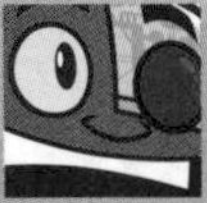

In between the pages. What? I can't be emotional just because I'm half machine? *Pshhh!* I'm complicated just like everyone else.

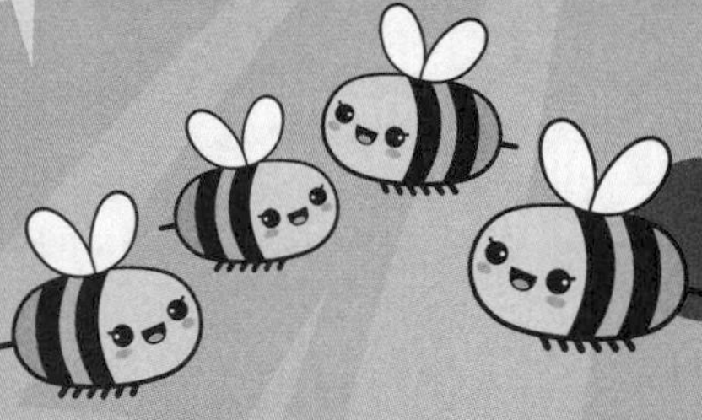

I am the simple.

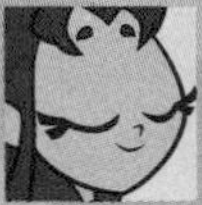

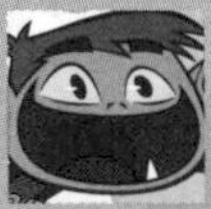

You ready to get this show on the road?

***Yeaaah*, I thought so.**

THE TEEN TITANS: WHERE ARE THEY NOW?

Where we've always been, fool. **RIGHT HERE.**

I can't think of any place I'd rather be than with you guys.

The bestest of the friends.

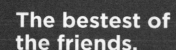

Till the end. Or whenever.

Titans TOGETHER!

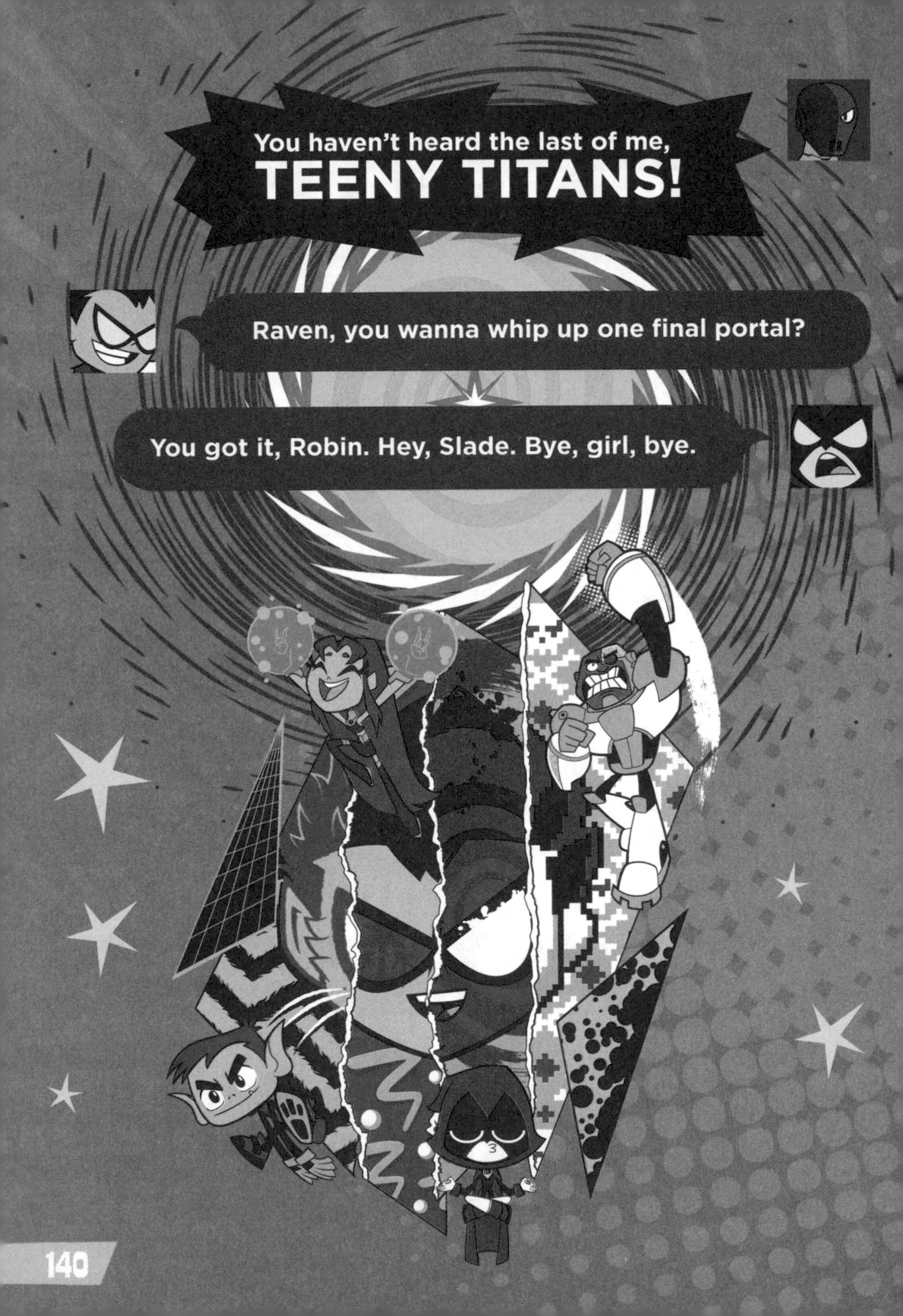
You haven't heard the last of me, TEENY TITANS!
Raven, you wanna whip up one final portal?
You got it, Robin. Hey, Slade. Bye, girl, bye.